'But why?'

Why couldn't it b███████████████████
the way? Because ████████████████ ~~like~~
that ... And while ~~she~~ suffered an anguished
uncertainty over their future Victor slept.
Christie's heart was tearing and he slept. Her
heart was raw with pain and he slept. She
wanted to die with the agony of it all and he
slept. She cried and he slept.

Dear Reader

As Easter approaches, Mills & Boon are delighted to present you with an exciting selection of sixteen new titles. Why not take a trip to our Euromance locations—Switzerland or western Crete, where romance is celebrated in great style! Or maybe you'd care to dip into the story of a family feud or a rekindled love affair? Whatever tickles your fancy, you can always count on love being in the air with Mills & Boon!

The Editor

Natalie Fox was born and brought up in London and has a daughter, two sons and two grandchildren. Her husband, Ian, is a retired advertising executive, and they now live in a tiny Welsh village. Natalie is passionate about her cats, two of them strays brought back from Spain, where she lived for five years, and equally passionate about gardening and writing romance. Natalie says she took up writing because she absolutely *hates* going out to work!

Recent titles by the same author:

A LOVE LIKE THAT
LOVE OR NOTHING
POSSESSED BY LOVE

ONE MAN,
ONE LOVE

BY

NATALIE FOX

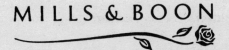

MILLS & BOON LIMITED
ETON HOUSE, 18-24 PARADISE ROAD
RICHMOND, SURREY TW9 1SR

First published in Great Britain 1994
by Mills & Boon Limited

© Natalie Fox 1994

Australian copyright 1994
Philippine copyright 1994
This edition 1994

ISBN 0 263 78451 7

Set in Times Roman 10½ on 12 pt.
01-9404-50949 C

Made and printed in Great Britain

CHAPTER ONE

'Excuse me, but would you mind turning that down?'

Christie was aware she was being spoken to, but stared stoically ahead at the headrest in front of her. Placido Domingo was coming nicely through her personal stereo and he was all she needed for a travelling companion.

Concorde was whisking her down to Barbados from Miami and she had enough on her mind without getting involved in trivial conversation. Her emotions were so muddled, torn between two people she loved very much: Paul and her beautiful cousin Michelle . . .

Suddenly her earphones were plucked from her head and a dark head jutted so close to her face that she would have reeled back if she'd had the room to.

That was the trouble with flying, Christie thought ruefully, you were a captive audience to whomsoever you were seated next to. There were no avenues of escape when a bore insisted on striking up a conversation when it wasn't asked for.

'I've already asked you politely to turn that contraption down, now I'll impolitely ask you to shut it!'

His voice was like hot gravel and his eyes murderously black. Christie stiffened rebelliously and snapped off the stereo.

'Thank you,' he grated in a suffering tone.

With a sigh of relief the bore sat back in his seat and carried on tapping out on his laptop computer.

Christie was annoyed, so annoyed that she broke her vow of silence.

'You know, there was a time when supersonic travel promised a better class of flight passenger——' she started bitingly, ready to give him a helping of vitriol for having the nerve to ask her to turn her stereo down when he was clattering away on his computer, but he interrupted her before she had a chance to add any more.

'Yes, life is full of disappointments,' he drawled meanly, not removing his eyes from that little grey screen on his lap. 'And the very idea that a personal stereo is personal is another of life's bitter disappointments.'

Now his eyes were up and across to her, dark, penetrating and quite, quite cold. A challenging look, though. Christie took it up with eyes just as dark and penetrating.

'You couldn't possibly have overheard——'

'Domingo.'

Christie swallowed, but held on to that gaze of his. Her lips turned up at the corners. He thought he was so smart.

'Clever guess,' she snorted, averting her eyes away from his to stare at the headrest again, a far more interesting subject. 'But I'm totally unconvinced.'

He let out a weary sigh. 'I thought you might be. Precision you want, precision you'll get, and then maybe I can have some peace to get on with my work. Verdi's *Aida*, "*Se quel guerrier io fossi*" . . . Celeste Aida, Act One.'

He *was* smart!

'Really,' Christie drawled sarcastically. 'You missed, "Accompanied by the New Philharmonic Orchestra".'

'I missed nothing because it was the Orchestra del Teatro alla Scala,' he told her in a low voice loaded with what-do-you-know?

Christie mentally squirmed in her seat, not giving him the satisfaction of the real thing. Not only was he a bore, but an opera buff to boot. She shut her eyes, because that was the only way out. So he had scored—bully for him. Let that be the end of it. Except she heard him mutter under his breath, 'And not even a smile from the lady.'

Christie didn't smile for airline bores. Her lips tightened even more and she heard a low laugh and then the tap, tap of his keyboard again.

The trouble was that now he had started it she was made to feel acutely aware of him seated next to her. Before he had been a nonentity; now he was someone with long, strong thighs, impeccable taste in designer wear, and a man who knew how to smell good. Something out of the Givenchy house, wasn't it? Just her luck to be seated next to the best-looking bore on the flight... Heavens, had she really noticed he wasn't bad-looking? She, who, after her disastrous relationship with Paul, had vowed she wouldn't allow herself to get into such an emotional mess ever again. Oh, no, she didn't want a man in her life, didn't need one, and she wasn't going to have one!

She felt a soft tap on her shoulder and opened her eyes to the BA stewardess smiling down on her. 'Champagne, Miss Vaughan?'

'I'm sure Miss Vaughan would be happy to join me in a toast,' came the voice next to her. He had the audacity to reach across her and take two glasses from the stewardess, so speeding her departure to the next traveller. He handed one to Christie with a very slight smile, baring a glimpse of white teeth that hadn't been manufactured in Florida, though the deep tan and the designer outfit screamed that they were.

She took the drink, because she needed it. 'And what are we toasting, your knowledge of Verdi's arias?' she suggested drily.

'You can toast what you like; I'm saying a thankful prayer for safe deliverance from a lingering death by boredom. Thank you for making my trip so silently rewarding. It's almost a pleasure to meet a woman who doesn't drone on indefinitely about everything that is a million miles from a man's heart.'

Christie tightened her already whitened fingers around her glass. Chauvinist creep. She wondered why some erstwhile female hadn't knocked out those home-grown teeth, because they were certainly a tempting proposition, especially after a wearisome trip from England when body and brain were flagging badly.

'The trick,' she murmured meaningfully, 'is never to start a conversation in the first place.' She hoped he'd take the hint that, now they were talking, it wasn't the green light to anything more.

'I know that trick too and usually adhere to it, but when you have a stereo blaster erupting in your left ear it's hard to stay mute for long.'

She afforded him a sidelong glance. He was gazing out of the window, and she was at the very least glad of that, but then he turned his dark head and met her deep brown eyes full on. Christie looked away. He was extremely attractive, Christie acknowledged. So there was life after Paul after all, she supposed; the fact that she could recognise an attractive man when she saw one proved that at least. But it would end with that recognition, because she certainly wasn't going to let it go any further than that.

'Barbados?' he queried, though not out of interest, Christie was sure. They had started and really there was nowhere else to go but onwards. They were nearly there anyway, and besides, she was going on from Barbados and it was extremely unlikely that he was too. He looked the sort of successful whatever who commuted down from Miami to Barbados on business every week. Probably a soft drinks salesman... No... that tropical suit was pure Armani... Maybe a Mafia man...? Hell, what did she care what or who he was?

'If not I'm on the wrong flight,' she clipped icily, then added, after a moment's flash of brilliance to end this before it went any further, 'I'm going to a wedding.'

She was used to being chatted up; Michelle said it was inevitable, with the Vaughan good looks inherited from their shared grandparents. Michelle thrived on it, which was peculiar in the circumstances of her impending marriage, and one of the reasons Christie balked at the thought of her marrying Paul. Michelle wasn't right for him; Christie was... or rather had thought she was.

'A wedding, eh?' came the now interested murmur next to her.

Christie sipped her champagne and lifted her chin. It was working. Lead with the hook and then slam in with the knee-buckler. She really didn't want to take this conversation any further. She settled back in her seat and, cradling the glass in her small fists, she closed her eyes once again.

'Yes, a wedding. A perfectly romantic wedding in paradise,' she murmured languidly. Now this should really shut him up for good. 'My own,' she added meaningfully.

Nothing from him, no comment, none whatsoever, which was what she expected and had hoped for, but her conscience rankled and spat and spluttered for the lie she had told. But a lie could be useful at times such as these, to get rid of an airline bore who had the audacity to tell her to turn her personal stereo down. She'd never see him again, so what was the harm? No one was going to get hurt by a little white lie. She *was* going to a wedding, one in paradise. That bit was true and the bit about it being her own *should* be true but agonisingly wasn't.

Pain... She was beyond the threshold of it after six months of soul-searching, and was now in a state of anguished limbo, wondering if Paul was truly, truly happy with her beautiful, flighty, happy-go-lucky cousin, who had so little to offer but her bubbly personality. She, Christie Vaughan, had had so much more to offer him. She had a successful career in broadcasting and a brain that wasn't swayed by... what was a million miles from a man's heart.

It had been hard coming to terms with it: the fact that Paul had thrown her over for Michelle. It was more than pride taking a jolt. She had honestly believed she and Paul had been right for each other, and to discover that she had entirely misinterpreted his feelings for her had shaken her so deeply that she wasn't over it yet.

That was love for you—blinding, incapacitating and most of the time a pain in the butt. At least she'd had a stab at it, though, which she supposed was something, but to lose him to her cousin, dear Michelle, whom she loved dearly, was a double hurt. She couldn't be allowed a satisfying stab of hate for the woman who had taken him from her. She had just stood aside and watched as their attraction to each other had blossomed into love, and now they were going to be married...and life was nothing but a bowl of rotting cherries.

She was on her feet and gathering up her magazines and stereo to ram into her shoulder-bag after they landed at Grantley Adams airport when he spoke again, her travelling companion.

'I wish you every happiness in your new life.'

She faced him, surprised at the low softness of his voice. She supposed he was quite a nice guy at heart, certainly a looker, and she almost wished she hadn't judged him so harshly. Only almost, though; he had a chill about him, almost a ruthlessness in those chiselled designer features and those piercing dark eyes. The comparison to Paul with his sun-bleached blond hair and ravishing, sporty open good looks was inevitable, she supposed. Her life seemed to be one of comparisons now that she had lost out on love. Paul and this man were exact opposites, absolutely exact, like black and white, Verdi and Duke Ellington, raw silk and comfortable fresh cotton. Paul was comfortable, this man tricky silk. Christie gave him a cool look.

'Thank you,' she murmured tightly.

He reached into the breast pocket of his not so raw silk shirt, took out a gold-edged card, and handed it to her.

'My card,' he offered with a hint of a smile hovering at the corners of his well defined lips.

Christie took it, because it was the only thing to do. She glanced at it with little interest, because that was the only thing to do too.

'Victor Lascelles,' she read out aloud, 'Attorney of Law.' She looked at him, raised a cool, dark brow, and handed it back to him. 'Fascinating, I'm sure,' she murmured with obvious boredom and uninterest.

He took the card and the smile widened, and with a slow, languorous movement he slipped it down into her cleavage as she bent to pick up her bag from the seat. His fingers were warm on that intimate part of her flesh and just for a split second they seemed to linger there as if in temptation, and then suddenly the touch was over and she wasn't sure it had happened, and yet the soft tingling it left was proof that it had.

Shocked, Christie straightened herself up and glared hotly at him, too shocked to extricate the card from where it now burned against her golden skin.

His smile was ever widening, ever mocking the outraged expression on her beautiful face. 'Always at your service, Miss Vaughan. Give me a call some time.'

Christie could hardly speak, and when she did her voice came out more like a screech than the dulcet tones she used so expertly on her broadcasting interviews.

'I doubt I'll ever have need of your services, Mr Lascelles, though if this flight had lasted a second longer I might have committed murder, but then again you would hardly be of any help, being dead yourself!'

A dark brow raised mockingly to match that mocking smile. 'I don't specialise in defending murderers, Miss Vaughan...'

'What do you specialise in, then? Parking offences?' she insulted bitingly.

'I specialise in what you might need in the future, Miss Vaughan—divorce.'

'Divorce!' Christie spat contemptuously, her hand gripping her bag so tightly that her fingers went quite numb.

'Yes, divorce. Quick, painless divorce. I do believe I'm facing a prospective client at this very minute.'

Burning with rage, Christie grazed back, 'I'm not even married yet!'

'But about to be, and I see trouble ahead for the pair of you. You, Miss Vaughan, are hardly brimming over with pre-marital anticipation. In fact I'd go as far as to say this proposed marriage of yours is on the rocks before it has even set sail.'

Christie couldn't believe what she was hearing. 'How dare you?'

No smile now; that was breezed away with the hot air that swept in from the open doors of the aircraft. 'I'm just trying to be helpful,' he offered sincerely. 'It's my job——'

'It's your job to put marriage down, is it?' she interjected angrily. 'Before...before it has even happened?'

'I put broken marriages to bed, sweetheart. All tucked up neatly with the covers turned down...' Even as he spoke his eyes darted up and down her narrow frame as if he might enjoy tucking her up in bed. They came to rest on her widened dark brown eyes. 'But prevention is always better than a cure. If I were you I'd think very carefully about this forthcoming wedding of yours. With my expert knowledge on marital matters, I'd say you weren't ready for such a deep commitment, so take my advice and let the poor man off the hook before it's too late for both of you.'

Wider and wider grew Christie's eyes, hotter and hotter grew the rage inside her. This raw-silk man was a chauvinist pig to the nth degree.

'You truly are a smart-mouthed litigating leech, aren't you? Well, let me tell you something: you know nothing!'

The very narrowing of his eyes challenged that statement. 'I know what I know—that a beautiful woman has sat next to me on this flight with more bound-up tension inside that perfumed cleavage than a scud missile, more biting sarcasm inside that sexy mouth than is good for her, and a white-hot rage that Vesuvius would challenge her for.' He smiled. 'Don't tell me it's repressed sexual anticipation for the nuptials, because you look worldly enough to have sampled them already.'

Christie's face went scarlet with outrage. On a sharp intake of breath she blurted hotly, 'You ... you bastard!' Never but never in her life had she been spoken to like this.

His smile was on the increase. 'I can afford to be,' he drawled as his hand came up to tilt her chin, which was tilted far enough anyway in hot defiance of this man. 'Good luck conveyances to your hapless intended. He needs it more than you do, I suspect.'

His thumb smoothed across her chin as if testing the quality of her skin, and then his hand dropped away.

He brushed past her for the exit and Christie stiffened and raged inside and pouted like a child. Furiously she snatched at the card still nestling in her breast and tore it to shreds. What an insufferable, hateful, disgusting man!

But life had its compensations, she supposed as she made her way to the hospitality suite to wait for her connecting LIAT flight to the island of Grenada, still shaken by the whole episode, still smarting from his mean frankness. The chance of seeing that deplorable man again in her life was as remote as the burning tropical sun dropping out of the sky to sizzle in the blue, blue Caribbean sea.

'Oh, God, I'm melting,' Christie puffed exhaustedly as Michelle hugged her tightly at Grenada airport. 'Some private jet got clearance before we did at Barbados and we missed our slot and then I'm sure the pilot defected to the beach for a leisurely swim and a lobster snack before take-off. There was I thinking Concorde would shorten the journey.'

'The buck stops at the Caribbean, Christie,' Michelle laughed happily as she led her towards a dusty white taxi. 'You'll have to wind down now and get used to the leisurely pace of life here. No one rushes anywhere; the tempo is so laid-back it nearly stops altogether. Now relax, you're here and that's all that matters.'

'Yes, I'm here,' Christie mumbled wearily as she sat back in the air-conditioned taxi, scooping her damp dark brown—once lush—hair from her hot brow. And she tried to relax, but Michelle's bubbly good humour was almost too much to bear.

'How was Miami? And New York? I don't know how you do it, Christie. Oh, the hotel is out of this world, just the most perfectly romantic setting for a wedding. Wait till you see what Paul has arranged. We're going to be married on the beach, under the palms at sunset, and we are going to party every night——'

'Where is Paul?' Christie interrupted, easing her damp silk shirt away from tense shoulders. The humidity was getting to her, *and* the thought that Paul hadn't bothered to accompany Michelle to the airport to meet her. It really hurt. She knew she shouldn't have expected it, but they were all so close that she had. The whole idea of this paradise wedding and honeymoon was for Michelle and Paul to surround themselves with all the people they loved for a wedding of a lifetime. Yes, Paul loved her, not in the way she wanted, but more his way—a just-good-friends love. But it hadn't been that way in the beginning, though on reflection she was able to see that the relationship had been pretty one-sided. But at the time Paul had appeared to be the attentive escort. Man meets woman, instant attraction, candlelit dinners leading to a weekend down at the Vaughan family home, Shorden Manor, in Dorset. Man meets her cousin Michelle, woman in love steps back, and retires graciously with a very stunned, bruised heart.

'Sunfish-sailing or snorkelling or rum-punching,' Michelle gabbled. 'All the other guests have arrived, so there is some merry-making going on, I can tell you.'

Christie closed her eyes, hardly able to comprehend that people had the strength for merry-making in this humidity.

How much easier it would have been to bear if Paul had fallen for a stranger. They would never have reason to see each other again. But Paul was marrying into the family and she and Michelle were close, almost like the sisters they didn't have because they were both only children. Though thank goodness, for pride's sake, they hadn't been so close that Christie had confided in Michelle how deeply she had felt for Paul. Michelle would never know, and this was going to be the most difficult assignment of Christie's life. She was going to have to put on a brave face, to smile when she wanted to cry, for she was going to be standing next to her dear cousin dressed as a maid of honour instead of in the bridal gown she ought to be wearing. And how would she feel when Paul slipped that platinum band on her cousin's finger? It would all be over then, truly over, a love lost forever.

'Hey, are you all right?'

Christie blinked open her eyes and managed a weak smile. They were pulling into the drive of the hotel, and Christie couldn't fully appreciate the luxurious beauty of the place. Her eyes felt gritty, her head was pounding with travel fatigue, and she ached for a cool shower.

'I just want to sleep forever,' she told her cousin as they stepped out of the taxi, Christie crumpled and travel-worn, Michelle exuberant, tanned and bouncy in flowing saffron silk, her red-gold hair dancing with shimmering highlights reflected from the sun. God, she looked so golden and happy, how a bride-to-be

should look. Would Christie be looking like that if
the roles were reversed? A stab of truth hit her at that
weary point. Christie Vaughan wouldn't be here if she
were marrying Paul. They would be married in her
local church down in Dorset, a traditional wedding
with a handful of close friends and family, and not
this alien razzmatazz, exotic though it was. It was quite
a sobering thought.

'No chance of that,' Michelle bubbled. 'I'll give you
five minutes to swoop into a bikini and then it's go,
go, go.'

'I'm afraid it's going to be no, no, no, Micky, dear,'
Christie told her firmly as the two girls linked arms
and padded across the marble foyer of the hotel to
Reception. 'I absolutely insist on a recovery period.
While you've been busy satisfying the residency period
leading up to your nuptials I've been working my way
halfway round the world to get here. I'll be fit for
nothing if I don't get some well earned rest.'

Michelle smiled understandingly. 'Yes, you're right
and I'm being selfish . . .' She stopped and turned to
Christie and hugged her impulsively. 'I'm so glad
you're here, Christie. If it weren't for you I wouldn't
be here, marrying Paul. You know we both love you
for bringing us together.'

Christie clung to her and closed her eyes in sufferance. The worst day's work of her life had been
taking Paul down to Shorden.

'Get your rest,' Michelle told her as she released
her, but her green eyes were twinkling mischievously.
'But you'd better be rested enough for the party tonight—steel band on the beach and lashings of seafood

and champagne to start the celebrations. Everyone, but *everyone* will be there, and if you're not there'll be trouble, I warn you.'

Christie watched as she floated across the marble foyer to the terrace which led directly on to the white, white sands of a palm-fringed beach. Christie could swear she was six inches off the ground in her elation.

'Buck up, Christie Vaughan,' she told herself. 'You could turn out to be the party pooper if you're not careful.'

A maid showed her to her private whirlpool suite, which was set apart from the main hotel. There was a group of them, facing the white beach and backed by lush, heavily scented tropical gardens with palms swishing in the hot wind. Each had a double bedroom, *en-suite* bathroom and spacious sitting-room leading on to a shaded patio area with steps down to another small terrace and the whirlpool. It was all very secluded and private, a perfect honeymoon suite, with the bright blue Caribbean sea and a cloudless sky beyond.

After the maid left, telling her to call Room Service if she needed anything, Christie stood by the open patio doors and breathed the fragrant air that wafted in from the gardens. The secluded whirlpool beckoned invitingly and Christie concentrated her thoughts on pure self-indulgence, because that was less painful than anything else. She stripped off her clinging silk shirt and her crumpled linen trousers, showered away the travel grime, and, still naked, walked through the suite, out to the pool, and plunged in. Five minutes later she emerged, five minutes after that she had downed a weak gin and tonic, and five minutes after that she was sound asleep on the huge double bed.

When Christie awoke later the sun was going down, filling the room with a burnt orange hue. It was humid and hot. She stretched lazily, like a sleek cat, and lay in the stillness, gathering her thoughts together. The scent of frangipani was in the room, and chirruping tree frogs suddenly broke the enveloping stillness. In the far distance the evocative sounds of a steel band hung in the air, and beyond that the swish of water on the shore. The sounds were blissfully exotic till a wild shriek of gaiety cut over them all and brought Christie back to earth. She stirred restlessly, rolled over on to her stomach, and clawed at the pillow. She didn't want to be here, damn it, she just didn't. Not like this, feeling the way she did, all knotted up inside and aching to the marrow with loss.

She forced those miserable feelings of self-pity out of the way, because if she dwelt on them for too long she would lose the nerve to step outside this suite and face life. Hunching into a thin cotton robe, she stood by the open patio doors and watched the sun go down. It was huge and fiery and plunged into the Caribbean sea, where it seemed to sizzle for a few seconds and then was gone to brighten someone else's day.

The tropical darkness came quickly and Christie moved about the room, switching on lamps. She poured herself a cold drink at the courtesy bar, added a slice of lime for zest, and sipped it as she brushed out her long dark hair and wondered what to wear. The maid had unpacked for her while she slept and she skimmed through the rail, chewing on the lime as she wondered. The white Indian cotton with the thin shoulder-straps was all she had the strength to wear. It was light and frothy and cool and she slipped it on and, barefoot, went out of the suite into the gardens and found a path which circled the other suites. The path branched into two. The one on the left was signposted to the hotel, but she took the right one, which led directly to the shore.

She stood on the warm beach, the longest stretch of moon-silvered sands she had ever seen in her life, and she had seen some on her travels. To the left of her the party on the beach was in full swing. The steel band was playing 'Island in the Sun' while a crowd of wedding guests were hysterically negotiating the limbo bar. Christie turned her eyes to the right and saw a long figure silhouetted on the shoreline, a man, kicking his feet in the sand and looking positively pensive. For a moment her heart leapt, thinking it was Paul with his hands plunged deep into his pockets, but it wasn't a stance Paul was familiar with; he never stood still long enough.

Christie wanted to be on that part of the beach, isolated and away from the madding crowd, but the spot was already taken by someone who looked as if he felt as she did. For a moment she felt twinned to him, united in a thoughtful, pensive mood, at one with the sea and the velvety Caribbean sky, very much alone. With a small intake of breath she squared her shoulders and swallowed the lump in her throat and headed towards the wedding revellers.

Paul was the first to sight her as she came across the sands. With a whoop he swept her into his arms and nearly crushed her to death.

'Darling, at last. We thought you'd never rise before the sun.'

He set her down on her feet, clasped her face in his hands, and kissed her full on the mouth. It was the sort of contact she didn't need, for need it was that rose desperately inside her. Even knowing she couldn't have him, she still yearned for him; even knowing the kiss was probably born out of a surfeit of champagne, she still allowed herself the bittersweet pleasure of enjoying it. But her pain and pleasure were cut short as her dear cousin leapt on them both, hugging them both together, the two people Michelle loved most in the world.

Together, the two people Christie loved most in the world whirled her into the gathering of revellers swarming on the beach like an army of inebriate ants. Most she knew; a smattering of American friends of Paul's she didn't. But, as was the way of Americans, she was their bosom friend in minutes. Their warmth and charm and their ease with people made her feel a lot better and she was soon clutching a brimming glass of champagne in one hand and a stuffed crab back in another. This was going to be a heavy, but heavy, week of celebrations, Christie thought wryly as she swigged her champagne in a desperate attempt to catch up on some of the exuberance.

'Where the hell is that mean cousin of mine?' Paul yelled to no one in particular. 'Some wretched best man he's turning out to be.' To Christie he directed,

'He's probably skulked off somewhere. My apologies, Christie, darling, the man is Mr unsociability personified.'

'Why apologise?' Christie laughed, thinking the man probably had good sense and taste to match her own.

'Because the best man and the maid of honour are supposed to get it together; that's traditional.'

Christie's heart floundered for a second. This she didn't need—to be matchmade at what was going to be a painful enough occasion as it was.

'There he is.'

Christie followed his gaze to the lone, pensive figure on the shore, who was now, slowly, coming towards them. He was barefoot and his hands were still plunged deeply into his pockets, his head bowed reverently as if the sand beneath his feet held the world's secrets. He was still in silhouette, a ghostly figure against the backdrop of a fiery sky.

Christie knew then, by a strange, intuitive feeling that drizzled down her spine like a lazy waterfall. Later she was to ask herself how she knew, but it was one of life's little mysteries, never to be solved, like the sight of the hot tropical sun dropping down into the Caribbean sea and seeming to sizzle in its own death throes.

'Victor!' Paul yelled at the top of his voice.

Christie went hot and cold all over, almost shivery and feverish, as she told herself she deserved this, and how she deserved it. It was a cruel punishment for a harmless little lie.

Life's bowl of rotting cherries was going for rapid fermentation, she thought dismally as she braced herself to meet the attorney of law who was going to be Paul's best man—the best man of the man Christie had loved and lost—at this perfectly romantic wedding in paradise. The wedding she had claimed as her own. Oh, misery, misery.

CHAPTER TWO

AT THE very least Christie admired him for not breaking into an eager trot at the sound of Paul's voice careering down the beach to bring his head up with a start. Then Paul was jogging, sportsman-like, over the sand to meet him, or, more than likely, to make sure he didn't escape.

It was one of the longest periods of Christie's life, watching them ambling towards her, Paul chatting eagerly, Victor dragging his feet as if he wished he weren't here at all, which she was sure was what he did wish.

'I know how he feels,' Christie murmured to herself, and turned away to join the crowd at the bar on the terrace, trying to melt in with them and not be noticed. The steel band broke into 'Yellow Bird' and the crowd shifted eagerly to the sand, breaking up into couples to gyrate themselves under the stars, leaving Christie on her own. She felt like the last crumbling party vol-au-vent that nobody wanted.

The beaming Grenadian waiter behind the bamboo beach bar topped up her glass of champagne with a theatrical flourish, and Christie's only thought for the moment, forced on her by way of a diversion to what was going to be a surfeit of embarrassment, was that this whole calabash must be costing Paul a fortune.

She heard laughter behind her—Paul's. She doubted if Victor Lascelles had a laugh in his body. Paul had

had time to fill in her CV of life to his cousin as they came across the beach to her, so she knew when she turned he wouldn't be surprised. Miss Vaughan of the Concorde flight down from Miami, Miss Vaughan of the rowdy personal stereo, Miss Vaughan going to a Caribbean wedding in paradise...dear God, her own.

Lawyers had a perceptive eye, this particular lawyer an above average perceptive eye. This Victor Lascelles would see right through her as if she were as full of holes as a rusty sieve. It would be pushing credibility too far to expect him to believe she was going on to her own wedding after this one. The man was certainly no gullible fool.

She was smiling, a dry, forced smile for appearances' sake, as she turned to face them: Paul, the man she had loved and lost, and Victor, the man who, because of sod's law, now knew her terrible secret—that this paradise wedding was wishful thinking on her part. But perhaps he didn't. She might be able to talk her way out of it. After all, it was part of her job when personalities on her broadcasting interviews tried to turn the tables on her when she asked tricky questions.

'Christie, how nice to meet you.' His penetrating dark gaze gave nothing away, nor the bland tone of his voice. No one would have guessed they had ever set eyes on each other before this moment. Only he and she and He up there knew that they had.

'I'm sorry, I can't shake hands,' Christie tried, in a voice as natural as she could make it. 'Champagne and crab backs.' She shrugged her shoulders and slightly raised her full hands to flippantly show him human contact was out of the question.

'It will have to be the continental way, then,' Victor said quietly, and his hands came to her shoulders, his head swooped down, and he kissed her on the cheek and then ... on the other one.

Christie's senses were whirled by a subtle hint of an exclusive cologne that she was very familiar with and the firmness of his lips on her heated skin, which she wasn't at all familiar with. She supposed the sharp awareness was brought about by a crippling embarrassment that she was doing her very best to disguise, because it certainly couldn't be anything else.

'Yeah,' laughed Paul, rather coarsely to Christie's over-sensitive ears, 'start as you mean to go on, say I.' Which, Christie thought, must have sounded somewhat coarse to anyone's ears.

Surely he hadn't been like that when she had known him? Had it only been six months since she had first introduced him to her cousin?

'Isn't he gorgeous?' Michelle screeched, appearing from nowhere to throw herself into Victor's arms and lean her red-gold head intimately against his shoulder, as if she had known him a lifetime.

It occurred to Christie that she did know him quite well. He was Paul's cousin, hadn't he said? Somehow that added to Christie's misery. Michelle was about to become part of Paul's family, something Christie would never be.

Christie forced an unabashed smile. 'Fascinating, I'm sure,' she said for Victor's ears only, a not very subtle reminder of a previous conversation.

Victor Lascelles picked it up immediately and his dark eyes glinted momentarily with humour, but then that glazed, uninterested look shifted the humour from

them, making Christie feel decidedly more uncomfortable than ever.

She knew then that the smart-mouthed attorney of
law was equally out of place in this pocket of paradise
as she was, though for very different reasons. Hers
she knew, painfully; his, she guessed, were simply that
he was a fish out of water, hauled in by his cousin to
perform a role which was aeons away from what he
did for a living, tucking up broken marriages.

In one way Christie was grateful for the noisy
revellers, because suddenly people were jostling at the
bar again, and if Christie was very clever she could
ease back, ease away, and flee to somewhere quiet to
think about how she could explain to her opera-buff
travelling companion that he must have misheard what
she had said on the flight down. No, of course I didn't
say I was going to my own wedding... Whatever gave
you that idea...? Must have been turbulence in the
airways! She remembered he had acute hearing and
was a wretched lawyer and could probably tell a liar
at fifty paces!

'The lambada!' Michelle shrieked, and dragged a
helpless Victor across the terrace to the steel band.

Relief swamped Christie. Now she could escape.
And yet she was torn for a brief second. She wondered if Victor Lascelles had hips that moved, and her
curiosity kept her rooted to the spot for a while. Stiff
as a board, she noted with uncharacteristic glee,
though he was certainly getting the hang of it.

Yes, he was quite a mover, she was forced to acknowledge to herself minutes later as she edged away
from the bar to make her escape. But then he would
be, wouldn't he? she thought ruefully as she headed

back to the scented garden, where the tranquillity of her private suite beckoned.

She awoke late the next morning to a blissful silence. The party the night before had racketed on till nearly dawn and Christie had seriously considered making up another fearful lie—that she had been called back to the UK for a world-exclusive interview with the Prime Minister or someone equally eminent.

She showered and dressed in a flowing mandarin silk pareu, tied her hair back for coolness, and braved the outside. She couldn't hide herself away; she had to face the world and more than likely suffer the scathing put-down by a certain lawyer. And he *would* put her down for that lie she had told; lawyers were trained to go for the jugular.

'May I join you?'

Christie's jugular throbbed as Victor Lascelles promptly dropped himself down in the cane seat across from her, under the welcome shade of a rippling palm-frond parasol on the breakfast terrace of the hotel. He wore cool linen trousers over the hips that moved, and a paprika-coloured silk shirt over the broad shoulders Michelle had provocatively draped herself against the night before.

'If I said no, would it make any difference?' she asked tartly.

She turned to the waiter and ordered rolls and coffee and stretched her bare legs under the table and stared out to sea. The blue-green of the ocean made her eyes ache with its sparkling brilliance.

'If you want me to sit elsewhere I will,' he said quietly after giving the same order to the waiter.

She flicked her eyes from the sea to him and was very surprised by that remark. She had fully expected a cavalier 'I'll sit where I damned well like' retort, though on reflection that thought was out of order. After all, he had initially asked if he might join her, and politely too.

'You're welcome,' she murmured, American-style. She looked around her, and everyone was conspicuous by their absence. They were the only breakfast diners on the terrace at the edge of the beach.

'The others have taken off on a sailing trip round the islands,' Victor told her.

She eyed him narrowly; perception he certainly had. 'Why didn't you join them?' she asked.

He looked at her as if the question wasn't worth the breath of answering. 'Why didn't you?'

'I would have done if I'd been asked,' she said truthfully, just a little peeved that no one had made the suggestion to her. She would have gone because this man across from her wouldn't have. He was a loner; she knew that after last night and that solitary stroll on the moon-bathed beach she had witnessed.

'I wonder why you weren't asked,' he murmured, gazing out to sea as if he wasn't really interested anyway.

He made her feel uncomfortable, because she had expected to be grilled about weddings. By now he must know why she was here. Maid of honour, what a hideous label to have hanging around her shoulders like a crocheted shawl, as if she *was* some old maid. As she watched a fringe of white sea curl over white sand she thought she probably would be some old

maid . . . well, at least some old career maid. That was
something; she might have lost her heart to someone
she couldn't have, but at least she had her career to
fall back on.

'Paul told me you did a couple of interviews on the
way down here. In New York and Miami.'

She marvelled at his ability to chart her thoughts.
'Just a couple of pilot shows,' she told him. 'For the
last three years I've worked in broadcasting, but now
I've joined a television company who are planning a
series of interviews with businessmen who've made it
big after a poor start in life. Rags-to-riches sort of
thing.'

'Perhaps you should interview me, then,' he said
with a small smile.

Christie raised her dark brows in surprise. He
noticed and his smile widened. 'I might be a cousin
of Paul's, but born the wrong side of the blanket, so
to speak. A true bastard.' His eyes locked into hers,
a blatant reminder that she had called him one. 'I had
to claw my way to success without the aid of the Tarrat
millions,' he stated frankly.

'Paul didn't exactly accumulate *his* fortune through
grovelling to his father,' Christie told him in defence
of Paul, though Victor was hardly attacking him for
being born with a silver spoon in his mouth, just
hinting at it. 'His property company is very successful
in its own right.'

'Helped by the right connections and plenty of back-
up if he had fallen flat on his face.'

'Yes, true,' Christie conceded. 'Are you bitter
about that?'

He gave her a strange look. 'No, did I give that impression?'

She shook her head. 'No, not at all, but you probably have reason to feel that way. The Tarrat empire is something to have to contend with, being born the wrong side of the blanket and all that.'

'No one can beat the feeling of having made it by their own efforts. It certainly would have helped to have a few strategic connections put my way, but they weren't and that was how it was and here I am, a self-made man who isn't obliged to suffer fools gladly.'

Christie smiled. She was beginning to like this Victor Lascelles ... well, his attitude at least. 'And yet you are here,' she murmured.

The waiter arrived, in no great hurry to serve them, but with such a bright smile across his face that he could be forgiven his slow-motion actions as he set the breakfast on the table.

As he ambled off Victor poured coffee for them both and asked, 'What do you mean by that?'

Christie broke a roll into pieces and spread it with ice-cold butter before it melted in the heat. 'You certainly didn't look happy to be here last night. In fact I'd go as far as to stay you looked as if you were hating it all.'

'I do hate it all. Any gathering of rich "what-shall-we-do-next-for-some-sport?" idlers, which most of them are, bores me to death.'

'That raw statement smacks of bitterness,' Christie told him.

'Not at all. I like what I like and this isn't it.'

'Yet you are accepting Paul's hospitality, drinking his champagne, drinking his coffee at this very minute.' Suddenly Christie let that small ball of liking for him roll out from her heart. All of this was being paid for by Paul, and though he could well afford it his generosity wasn't in question, but some people's attitudes were. Victor Lascelles's, for instance. If he felt so strongly about it he shouldn't be here accepting it.

'I'm not a free-loader, Christie. Are you?'

Christie bridled at the suggestion. She swallowed a piece of roll before snapping back at that.

'No, I'm not. Michelle is my cousin and I love her and we are close, and that is the only reason I'm here.'

His eyes dragged over her, questioningly, suspiciously, judiciously. 'Is that the only reason?' he said softly.

He knew, Christie was sure of it, and he was going the long way about getting to what he obviously wanted to thrash out with her—why she had claimed this wedding was hers.

'We were talking about *you* and why you offered your best-man services to someone you obviously despise in a situation you admitted you loathe,' Christie protested.

'My services weren't offered, they were requested, and I didn't say I despised my cousin. I'm very fond of him—man to man, you understand.' His eyes twinkled very slightly at that. 'But I certainly have little time for his noisy friends and yes, it's true, I loathe the situation. I can think of nothing worse than embarking on supposedly wedded bliss with half the hooray Henry set quaffing exorbitantly expensive champagne on the shores of an alien paradise at my expense and sailing off into the sunset expecting the blue bird of happiness to sing forever on the front porch of life from then on.'

Christie burst out laughing.

'Have I said something funny?'

Christie, shaking her head with laughter, topped up her coffee and his too. She couldn't be angry with him, because he voiced what she thought herself.

'No, not funny really, just a bit sad. I won't argue with you, Victor, because everything you say is true to my own heart. But the difference is I'm a romantic at heart, and all this isn't my style either, but I wouldn't knock other people for doing it. It obviously turns them on. You're certainly not a romantic. Too much of your work has rubbed off on you. Are you here because you think this marriage we are discussing won't work? Victor the vulture, waiting to peck at the carrion of another doomed marriage.'

He didn't say a word, not one. He sipped his coffee and watched her studiously over the rim of his cup.

Christie wondered if that remark had hurt him, but dismissed the thought. He was too tough to be hurt. She apologised none the less. 'I'm sorry,' Christie murmured in a low voice. 'That was a bit below the belt.'

'Apology accepted,' he said quietly and put his cup precisely back in its saucer. He leaned back and suddenly Christie felt threatened, but she couldn't put a finger on why she felt that way.

'So why are you here, Christie? Intuition tells me you are hardly looking for a freebie yourself. You wear expensive clothes, you smell expensive, you travel expensive. You aren't one of the crowd. You looked as if you were hating it all last night as well and you've admitted it isn't your style, so why?'

Her heart contracted. Here it comes, she thought.

'You know why. I've just told you. Michelle is my cousin. I'm her maid of honour. I'm here for exactly the same reason as you are, a family wedding.'

'I don't think that is all the story, Christie.'

'I'm not a liar!' It was out before she could stop it, the heated statement of denial of something he knew not to be true.

He smiled thinly and his eyes hit their target—hers. 'Now we both know you are, so that was a silly thing to say, wasn't it?' He spoke to her as if she were a child.

'Don't patronise me!' she seethed through tight lips.

She went to get up, but his hand shot out and clamped over her hand on the table.

'You can't do that in a television studio, you know, just run when it all gets too hot. Front it, Christie. Tell me something that will make me believe you're different from most of the silly females I meet.'

Christie snatched her hand back from under his and glared furiously at him across the table. 'Easy to see why you are what you are and so successful at it. I bet the female of the species never comes out of your divorces with custody of her pride!'

She stood up then, because paradise was turning very sour on her. The man was a misogynist and she wasn't willing to become one of his targets for derision.

'Thanks for your company at breakfast. I shall do my best to avoid you at lunchtime *and* dinner tonight.

In fact I'll do my best to avoid you till the very day we have to meet at the wedding ceremony.'

'The wedding ceremony you claimed as your own?' he questioned drily, leaning back in his seat to deliver it, knowing he had her cornered.

Boy, he didn't give up. Christie leaned towards him, her palms on the table to steady herself, and she needed steadying, because what she really wanted to do was readjust his features for him. 'One of my tactics for getting rid of airline travelling bores,' she told him scathingly.

He was totally unconvinced and that penetrating gaze of his told her so before his lips spoke the words. 'Liar. I think it was wishful thinking on your part. Of course I didn't know that at the time, but now I know a little more about you, thanks to the loose tongue of your ex-lover, my cousin Paul.'

Christie's insides went hot and cold simultaneously. God, but they had never reached the point of being actual lovers. Surely Paul hadn't boasted that they had been? But men were men . . . but not Paul. He couldn't have said that, could he?

'What . . . what has he told you?' she stammered, her mind flashing that this could all be a very dangerous situation. She had loved Paul and they'd had a relationship before Michelle, not a sexual one, though she had thought they were getting close to it, but she didn't want the world to know. What on earth had induced Paul to tell his cousin they had once been lovers?

Slowly Victor Lascelles stood up. He delved into his pocket for some notes to throw on the table for a tip for the breakfast waiter. Christie, frantic to divert her thoughts in another direction, stared at the notes he threw down. The lawyer certainly wasn't a mean man where tips were concerned, but mean could mean something meaner. Was he punishing her for that lie she had told to try and fool him? He'd said he didn't suffer fools gladly.

'Paradise can go to the head, Christie,' he said solemnly. 'Remember that over the next few days.'

'What the hell do you mean by that?' she blazed in confusion. She hadn't a clue what he was getting at, and she badly wanted to know as it obviously concerned her.

'I've said enough,' he said, tight-lipped. 'Now would you like to join me for a swim in the Caribbean or the hotel pool maybe? The others won't be back till supper tonight and the tropical days can be long.'

'I'd rather swim with the sharks than you!' Christie blurted, furious he wouldn't open up to her further and explain that cryptic warning.

'I'm sure you'd be in good company, then,' he drawled and gave her a wide smile. 'Have a nice day.' He turned and sauntered off towards the gardens, leaving Christie burning with curiosity and rage.

Much later that day she heard the hotel come alive again as a convoy of taxis deposited the wedding guests back at the hotel, and then there was a silence till sundown as the happy revellers slept off the rest of a day of quaffing on the high seas, gathering their strength for another evening's offering of high-spirited entertainment.

Christie had spent a lazy but disturbing day mulling over everything Victor Lascelles had said at breakfast and mulling over all she had lost with Paul. Even now she still couldn't fathom out what had gone wrong. He had been so attentive with phone calls and wining and dining her and then it had all gone wrong when she had introduced Michelle to him.

Paul had been swept off his feet, and, though Christie told herself a hundred times that if he'd truly cared for her that couldn't have happened, she still felt that it was a lot to do with her not opening up her true feelings to him. She had just taken it for granted that he felt the same way and had been deeply shocked to find that obviously he hadn't. And the aftermath of the whole painful business was this feeling that she was obviously not cut out for love because she had handled it so badly.

But surely when you had a relationship with someone, when you had given your heart to someone, they should know without your having to spell it out in capitals? But Paul's friends and business associates were high-flyers, taking what they wanted without a thought for the romances of life. It hurt her deeply that Paul should have thought of their relationship as a passing fancy, and it was obvious he had, because he had mentioned it to his cousin so lightly, almost boastfully, considering the exaggeration of it.

Christie heard a tap at her door as she was making herself a drink as the sun was going down. She was surprised it was Paul when she answered it.

'Looks like I'm just in time to join you for a drink.' He stepped into the suite and slumped down into one of the pastel-covered sofas that furnished the cool, spacious room.

'You look exhausted,' Christie laughed as she poured him a large gin and tonic.

'Life is exhausting,' he breathed, taking the glass from her. 'But you look as ravishing as ever, so what have you been doing all day in our absence?'

It suddenly occurred to Christie that she hadn't been invited on the mini cruise with them because it had been hoped she would team up with Victor for the day. Paul and Michelle matchmaking? She repressed a shudder at the thought.

'Still unwinding,' she told him, flopping down into the sofa across from him.

He smiled. 'Thought so. It's why we left you alone for the day. You looked exhausted last night and left early, so we guessed you were still jet-stressed.'

That was a relief at least, that everyone was concerned with her health and nothing else. 'Thoughtful of you, and there was I thinking you were trying to foist your cousin Victor on me.'

He laughed and her heart tugged, because his charm when he smiled like that was what she had first been attracted to.

'Last night was just a suggestion to warm the party up. Victor doesn't communicate very well with the opposite sex. He's no parish priest by any means, but he doesn't let women get under his skin. Hasn't time for them. Work is his driving force, as many have discovered at their cost. I wouldn't foist him on my worst enemy, Christie, and you are definitely not my worst enemy.'

For a second he held her eyes above the rim of his glass as he held it to his lips, and that quick perusal had a strange effect on Christie. She felt an odd unease creep down her spine and wondered if she had misinterpreted the look. Like Victor, she too had a certain talent for perception, and that look had definitely... no, she was mistaken.

'Where's Michelle?' she asked quickly.

'Next door with Victor. He's trying to cry off the party tonight, claiming pressure of work; he lives for it. Michelle will talk him out of it.' He paused to drain his drink and then when he spoke again that funny feeling down her spine was there again. 'Her powers of persuasion are next to none,' he added quietly.

Christie watched him thoughtfully, wondering why she had the feeling that something wasn't quite right here. Paul didn't look his usual self. 'Slightly jaded' was probably a fair description of him at this moment. But then he'd had a hectic day sailing the high seas. No, there was something more, and she didn't know what, which made her think she wasn't so bright at being perceptive after all.

'Another drink?' She got up from the sofa and Paul held his empty glass up to her. His smile was crooked this time and there was that funny look in his eye again.

'Perfect,' he murmured. 'It's so relaxing with you, Christie.'

Poor love, Christie mused, Michelle was running him ragged. By the time she had mixed fresh drinks at the courtesy bar by the open patio doors and turned to hand one to Paul he was sound asleep on the sofa.

She looked down on him for a few seconds, allowing herself the painful yet inevitable thought that things could have been so different if she hadn't taken him down to Dorset that fateful weekend. But it was

done and she had coped and she wished them both
every happiness, though she had learned a very
valuable lesson by it all. This relationship thing, she
really wasn't very clever at it and didn't want a go at
it again. Caution... It was a nice word; she'd
practise it.

An hour later Paul called out to her as she was
stepping out of the shower. She thought she was in
danger of showering herself away to a shadow, but
the heat was so oppressive that it was the only way
to stay sane. Christie wrapped a towel around her and
went into the bedroom, and Paul was standing in the
bedroom doorway, leaning against the door-jamb.

Her wet hair was dripping on her bare shoulders
and water from her long legs was trickling to the
marble floor. Paul was motionless as he watched the
droplets forming tiny puddles at her feet.

Christie stood rooted to the spot, puzzled for a
second by the strange look in his eyes again. Slowly
those pale eyes came up the length of her body to
meet her own. Insight was as sharp as a double-bladed
knife as she suddenly interpreted that look.

'Thanks for the respite care, Christie,' he said softly.
'See you at dinner.'

The Caribbean wind caught the front door as he
went out and it slammed so hard that the noise jarred
through the whole of her body, the body that was
now shaking from head to toe. This couldn't be
happening, she thought feebly. She thought she knew
Paul, but that look in his eyes as he had watched the
water dripping from her hair and legs was not one of
marvel at the laws of gravity. She had seen desire in

those clear blue eyes, a desire for her that she had never seen before.

Feverishly sweeping the offending wet hair from her face, she dismissed the very idea from her head. 'Respite', he'd said, respite from the pressures of the pre-wedding festivities; that was all she was. He had dropped into her suite for a drink with an old friend to get away from the crowd. But she wasn't an old friend, she was an ex-girlfriend—not even an ex-lover as he had suggested to Victor—but nevertheless . . . no, it was impossible, totally impossible.

Christie wandered the floodlit gardens before joining the others for dinner. She didn't want to join them at all, but avoidance was impossible. Fireflies danced ahead of her and she was watching them with such deep fascination that she didn't see Victor Lascelles till he was almost on top of her. They were on the edge of the gardens, where the sand spilled under hibiscus and yuccas and oleander, trying to tempt them down to the shoreline.

'I warned you, didn't I?' he said as their feet sank into warm sand as they headed towards the main hotel.

'I don't remember any warnings.'

'There was only one, about paradise going to the head.'

'That was a warning, was it? I thought you were making a weak attempt to sound profound,' she stated flatly, playing innocence.

'The intonation of my voice should have told you it was a warning.'

Christie shrugged. 'So now I know it was, but I fail to see what it was a warning against.' She stopped by a group of swaying palms and faced him. The moonlight was powerful and she could see every dark feature of his face. 'So are you going to tell me what the warning is all about?'

'I thought you would know by now.'

'Well, I don't.'

'You surprise me. I would have thought with your interviewing insight you would have picked up on what I was getting at.'

Christie felt those strange stirrings of disquiet once again, but didn't really know what they were about. 'I don't know what you mean,' she murmured.

He smiled for the first time. 'Private suites are another of life's bitter disappointments. I'd put them in the same category as personal stereos that aren't very personal.'

'I thought lawyers were famed for getting straight to the point. You certainly aren't. If you have something to say, spit it out before I grow grey hairs waiting.' Her voice was sharp and to the point and she hoped he'd play the same game.

Christie leaned back on a palm tree that in its infancy had been struck down by a persistent Caribbean wind and was now growing on the horizontal.

Victor Lascelles's left foot came up beside her on the unfortunate palm and he leaned towards her, so close that she felt his warm breath on her cheek.

'I wonder if you dealt with Paul this afternoon in such a direct way in your suite,' he said meaningfully.

Christie hid her surprise and smiled. 'Aha, now I see what you mean. Private suites aren't so very private. So you know Paul was with me for a while and I know Michelle was with you because Paul told me, so what sort of a case can we make out of that?'

'Michelle stayed long enough to persuade me to come to the party tonight—a very persuasive lady—and then she left. Paul stayed long enough with you to have tongues wagging. I rest my case.'

So he'd heard the slam of the door as Paul had left. 'You have no case,' Christie bit back, staggered he could think such a thing, but lawyers were always suspicious, she supposed.

'I have a very substantial case, Christie. You and Paul were once emotionally involved——'

'Once,' Christie emphasised strongly.

'And you wish you still were,' he suggested meaningfully.

Christie narrowed her eyes at him, her heart beating inside her for what he was suggesting, for what he was thinking of her.

'You know, if that suggestion weren't so offensive it would be laughable. Nothing happened this afternoon!' Christie protested.

'That is neither here nor there. You might have done something or you might not have done. But the fact is you were together, for quite an interesting length of time.'

Christie opened her mouth with shock then snapped her lips together to speak. 'That is a disgusting suggestion . . . that you think——'

'It's not important what I think. What I know is far more interesting.' He moved his foot back down to the sand, but was still so close to her that she could feel his unsettling heat. 'All that repressed aggression down on the flight from Miami, the lie about this being your wedding, the way you can't hide your feelings for your ex-lover, who is about to be married to your cousin... I'd say you were a pretty knotted-up young lady, so knotted-up you might think of trying to win him back before the event. Paradise can certainly go to your head, Christie Vaughan, and this is where my warning comes into being. Leave him alone. You can't win him back and you shouldn't try. Too many people might get hurt in the selfish process.'

Christie couldn't speak for the anger and the injustice that welled inside her. No words of denial could ever land on anything but stony ground with this man. Now she knew what his devious mind had been hinting at at breakfast that morning. He thought she was here to make a last desperate play for her lost lover.

To her horror his hand came up and he gripped her chin and held it, and the feel of his flesh on hers was so electrifying that she felt earthed to the spot.

'You are a very beautiful woman, Christie, a sore temptation to any man. I'm even tempted myself to sample the delights you have so willingly placed on offer to my cousin, but that would be playing dirty on my part, and two wrongs don't make a right. Nevertheless, paradise is a cruel tormentor, the heat and sun a great arouser of passion, so be warned.'

Then his arm came around her narrow waist, drawing her hard against him, and his mouth swooped down to hers and encompassed her lips so soundly and completely that she didn't have a chance to reel back with shock.

The kiss was powered by nothing but a grim emphasis of what exactly he thought of her and delivered with the skill of one who wasn't too choosy.

It did nothing for Christie's honour, nothing for his either, but all the same she was powerless to move a muscle to get out of his lip space. His grip on her was fierce and yet sensuous, drawing her against the full length of his body where it was possible to touch. She felt every muscle, every pulse pressed hard against her, the thud of his heart against her breast. She felt his strength and his need and it so fazed her that she felt her own need stir deeply within her. She was shocked by the quickening inside her, almost disgusted at her weakness for a man she didn't even like very much. She wanted the kiss to end, but a part of her didn't, and that aroused more disgust inside her.

He drew back first and she expected some sort of triumphant sneer to slide across his mouth, but instead he placed a warm kiss on her brow and then released her so sharply that she staggered back against the palm.

He walked away, heading down to the edge of the water, but at an angle so he would eventually end up at the hotel, where the soft strains of a small band were drifting heavenwards.

Christie stood watching him till her eyes filled with such stinging tears of rage that she couldn't see him any longer. She hated him for that—the heated punishment to her lips—and she hated herself for not stopping it, but worse, that blush of a kiss on her brow was the worst remonstration of all. It was as if he felt sorry for her.

And she should be pitied, she supposed as she brushed the tips of her fingers across her eyes to disperse the tears, pitied for allowing herself to get into this emotional state in the first place.

Victor Lascelles was wrong to think she would do anything to try and encourage Paul back to her. Never, never would she do that. But the pity of the thing was that Victor wouldn't believe her even if she tried to convince him she wasn't that sort of woman. She had loved and lost, had accepted her loss, and was living with it. Now she had a new pain to suffer—Victor's awful accusations and warnings and his way of emphasising them. Funny, but she should hate him for that, and a bit of her did, but the rest of her cried out for him not to think ill of her. And that was funny, verging on the hysterical. What the hell did she care what he thought? But she did. It really mattered, and that wasn't really funny at all.

CHAPTER THREE

IT WAS a much less hectic night than the one before. The hotel had laid on a beautiful and sumptuous buffet on the terrace, with its centrepiece an ingenious ice sculpture of a peacock in full courting display. Surrounding it were fat red lobsters, crab backs, king prawns and piles of spicy roti. There were marinated chickens, roast legs of lamb and beef, and every Caribbean fruit and vegetable, including mangoes and plantain, okra and yams.

Christie feasted her eyes, but that was all. The others just feasted. She had no appetite, but accepted a rum punch from the bar and sat on a coral wall away from the crowd. She'd intentionally isolated herself from the others because she couldn't get out of her mind what Victor Lascelles thought of her and the way he had shown his contempt by kissing her that way. Somehow it outweighed the rest of the misery she felt at being here.

She watched him, the man who thought so ill of her, averting her eyes every time there was a danger of him noticing her cool perusal. He seemed to have melted that cool reserve of his and was mingling with the others in a very relaxed way this evening. Probably touting for business, she mused spitefully. She wondered what sort of a love-life he had, this apparent paragon of virtue. Certainly some of the women guests weren't paragons of virtue. They abandoned partners and husbands at regular intervals to sidle up to him and flutter their eyelashes indiscreetly.

Christie supposed there was some truth in what he had said about the heat and sun and paradise. It seemed to loosen people's inhibitions, arouse their passions. There was certainly a lot of female interest in the tall, dark lawyer, but not a lot coming from him, and she supposed what Paul had said about him was true: no woman got under his skin. He seemed to have a built-in immunity to what paradise could do to the emotions, apart from what he had done to her by the palm tree on the way here. Derision seemed to be the only passion paradise aroused in him.

For the first time Christie noticed Michelle wasn't here, and when Paul joined her with a plate piled to overflowing and sat next to her on the wall she asked him where she was.

'Too much sun and champagne, though she said she'll join us later when she's rested.'

Christie stood up with concern. 'I'll go and see how she is.'

Paul's free hand snaked out and pulled her back to sit next to him. 'No need, she's spark out. You're not eating, Christie.'

Christie raised her rum punch to her lips and as she sipped the drink she was aware of Victor Lascelles watching them from the other side of the terrace. Heat invaded Christie's already damp skin, because she could imagine what was going through his mind. She hoped that he'd seen Paul approaching *her* and knew that she hadn't approached *him*.

'I'll have something later,' she murmured.

'No, you won't, you'll have something now.' Paul put his plate next to him on the wall, picked up a prawn, and started stripping the pink shell from it. 'I know you women, thinking calories all the time. Here, open your mouth.'

The prawn was at her lips before she could stop him. It was instinct to open her mouth to receive it, and an instinct she regretted instantly. Paul's eyes had darkened as her lips had parted . . . and . . . and Victor was still watching them.

Christie swallowed the prawn whole; it didn't even touch the sides. Another was at her lips before she knew what was happening. She laughed out of pure embarrassment. 'I'm not a child, Paul. I'm quite capable of feeding myself.'

'But it's not half as much fun,' Paul said in a low voice.

It was then that Christie saw all the danger signs flashing in neon. They hit her with a force that nearly crushed the air from her lungs. She now fully understood the disquiet she had felt that afternoon when Paul had come to her suite. She *had* seen desire in his eyes. Dear God, but Michelle wasn't here and . . . and her betrothed was feeding her so sensually . . .

'D-delicious.' Her voice sounded choked to her own ears. Shakily she got to her feet. 'You've whetted my appetite . . .' Oh, God, what a terrible choice of words.

Paul laughed softly. 'That was the idea,' he said smoothly, and suddenly his fingers were on the bare skin of her arm, caressing her inflamed flesh, though she wasn't inflamed with desire. The very opposite!

'I'd better get some food,' she said haltingly, and turned away. Her legs were so weak and senseless that she could hardly stumble to the buffet table.

Paul didn't follow and she was eternally grateful for that. Her breath was shaky as she grabbed a plate and started to pile food on it.

'You can't eat that.'

She whirled to face Victor, who was suddenly beside her. He was smiling knowingly, infuriatingly knowingly to Christie's eye.

'I eat what I like,' she blurted irritably.

Victor took the dyed onion from her plate and Christie stared at it stupidly, her skin going the same colour as the onion. It was a huge pink onion shaped into a beautiful floret, obviously sculptured by the same team that had sculpted the beautiful ice peacock that towered over them.

'It's a table decoration, not for human consumption,' he told her tightly. He settled the onion back into its display, picked up a server, and proceeded to pile her plate with food that was more appetising and edible. 'Here, try these prawns.' His voice was barely above a whisper. 'Let me peel them and feed them to you. I liked what I saw just then. Very sexual, very tempting——'

'Shut up!' Christie breathed furiously.

'Keep your voice down. Do you want everyone to know?'

'To know what? To know what you are obviously thinking?' she hissed under her breath.

'I saw what I saw and I know what I know. But it would be dangerous for others to have the same knowledge. Is that enough for you?'

She suddenly realised that his other hand was over hers as she held the plate. He was steadying her, stopping the trembling of her hand. If he let go of the plate she knew it would crash to the tiled terrace, and that would certainly attract attention. She drew on every reserve of strength she possessed to steady herself.

'More than enough. You can let go now,' she told him stiffly.

'Good, now let's go and find a nice quiet corner,' he suggested in that dark, warm, patronising tone of his. 'Somewhere out of harm's way where I can dish out another word of warning to you, because you obviously haven't heeded the first one I issued you with.'

Her strength went then, because this was so one-sided and unfair. If she protested her innocence he wouldn't believe her anyway and she couldn't tell him what she believed of Paul—that he was flirting with her. She could have been wrong about Paul, but she didn't think she was. He had definitely been . . . but definitely been what? she pondered miserably as she allowed herself to be led away to the perfumed gardens by Victor. Paul had come to see her in her suite this afternoon, fallen asleep, dazedly woken up and given her that strange look as she had dripped in front of him. And just now he had come to sit with her, because why not? They were friends, weren't they? And the business of his feeding her was just a bit of harmless fun, wasn't it? Oh, God, she prayed it was.

'Here will do,' Victor said. 'Sit down and eat and I'll go back to the bar and get us a couple of drinks. You won't run away, will you?'

Christie sat down on a bench flanked by creamy oleanders and looked up at him. 'I will if you keep on speaking to me as if I were a child or an undisciplined puppy,' she said tightly.

'Until you prove to me otherwise there will be no change in my attitude to you. Think on that while I fetch the drinks.'

Christie did think on it as he disappeared through thick, lush foliage. Her first reaction was flight back to her suite, but suddenly she had the feeling that that wasn't the safest place to be. Paul might come looking for her, Victor too. She didn't know who she feared most; all she did know for sure was that she was hating the lawyer for thinking what he did about her.

She stared down at the food on her plate. She was hungry, she realised, but had overlooked an implement to eat with. With her fingers she picked at the salad while she waited for him to come back.

'Try this,' he said, holding a fork out to her. He held two glasses of wine by the stems with the other hand as he sat down next to her.

'Thanks,' she murmured, taking the fork from him.

He put her wine down on the path at their feet. 'So why didn't you run?'

'Because I'm not a child or a puppy or what you think I am.'

'You don't know what I think you are.'

'You've made it quite obvious you think I'm still interested in Paul and you think I'm encouraging him too, and that is the main reason I'm still on this bench waiting for you. I don't like being judged before I've had a chance to state my case.'

He leaned forward, his elbows resting on his knees, his wine glass cradled in both hands. 'Go on, then.'

'Go on with what?' Suddenly she didn't want to talk about it, because it was so painful for so many different reasons and excruciatingly embarrassing as well.

'Say something that will convince me that you are not making a last-ditch attempt to get your lover back.'

She could have snapped back that it was none of his business, but that would be childish. She was angry, but held it back. She picked up a roti with her fingers and munched on it before speaking. She had this power to divert hurt to indifference, a trick she had learnt since that weekend in Dorset when she had lost Paul to Michelle.

'These are delicious. Have you tried them?'

He turned his face to look at her, and there was a half-smile on his face. 'Are you trying to pervert the course of justice by changing the subject?'

'Probably,' she said lightly, finishing the small pastry envelope of curried meat and vegetables and going on to lick her fingers.

'Don't you want to talk about it?' he persisted.

Of course she did if it meant he wouldn't think so badly of her. But really he was a stranger, so why should she care? And he was hardly likely to believe her anyway, so why fight for it?

'Is there any point? I mean, you've already made up your mind about me.' She leaned down and picked up her glass of wine.

'I haven't quite, as it happens.'

'That's a bit of a contradiction. Just now you said you know what you know and you saw what you saw.'

'I don't know your side of it, though, and it's only fair to give you a hearing.'

Christie shrugged dismissively. 'I feel condemned already, so what is the point in proclaiming my innocence?' She stared down at the path rather than look at him. She knew she was sounding contrary, very female to his chauvinist ears, but she wasn't ready yet to open up to him. Fear of more derision was holding her back.

'You'd be a push-over in court, then. Case dismissed because of lack of evidence.'

'You do contradict yourself a lot,' she retorted. 'You have the evidence. You're the chief witness for the prosecution. Guilty, so hang her on the strength of your evidence alone.'

'Do you conduct your interviews in this way? If you do they must be incredibly boring and one-sided.'

She looked at him and he was smiling, and she smiled back because she must be sounding very immature indeed. 'So what do you want to know?'

'Why you want him back.'

'I don't,' she told him truthfully. Strange that, but she didn't, and yet twenty-four hours ago she had been wondering how she could face life without him. But what had happened since her arrival had scared her.

'It certainly doesn't look that way.'

'Not to you it doesn't, because you have that sort of suspicious mind. If Paul hadn't told you that once we were lovers you wouldn't be giving me the third degree now.'

'Not on that alone I wouldn't, you're right, but don't forget we travelled down from Miami together.'

'Not together, Victor. We happened to be seated next to each other on the flight, that was all. If you hadn't heard my Walkman and told me to turn it off we would never have spoken, I wouldn't have told you that silly lie, and you wouldn't be thinking I'm trying to get my lover back.'

'But that lie came about not to shut me up, as you said, but from a deep-seated psychological desire for it to be your own wedding. I was right about your pent-up emotions. You were as tightly wound-up as a spring on that flight. Now the only reason for that is that this wedding was going to be very stressful for you, and the only reason for that is that you still love him. Women in love do strange things, sometimes alien to their true character, and with the heat and the sun——'

'Yeah, yeah, you've drummed that home to me enough times.'

'And yet still you don't heed my warnings,' he said in a gravelly voice.

Christie sat, thoughtful, and sipped her wine.

'So you are still in love with him?' he persisted.

She gave it serious thought before replying, but sometimes serious thought didn't help. Up until her arrival on this island she had thought she was still in love with him. Now she knew she wasn't, because Paul had frightened her, though fear wasn't quite the right word for how she felt, but it was near enough. She wasn't actually afraid of him, but maybe just afraid for the confusion he roused in her. Paul was flirting with her and that wasn't right and it wasn't fair, to her or anyone else, and yet she couldn't feel angry about it and she should, simply for the moral reason that it just wasn't on. No, it was this wretched confusion that was the main bother. Why on earth should Paul flirt with her when he was about to be married?

'Funny, but I don't think I can answer that.' She smiled enigmatically. 'I mean, love isn't as easy as that.'

'You either do or you don't.'

'That's all very well in theory, but practice is a much trickier thing to deal with. I thought I was in love with him, yet I let him go very easily, so therefore did I really love him enough? I should hate him for not realising that my feelings for him were deeper than he thought, but I don't. Hate should be another deep emotion that goes with love, especially when you lose it. I'm not even jealous of my own cousin, but on the other hand I envy her. Is any of this making sense?'

He shook his head solemnly. 'None whatsoever, but then the female mind always confused me. From a man's point of view I'd say love was black and white. You love or you don't. No confusion.'

'Have you ever been in love?' She laughed quickly and went on, 'Crazy, but I don't even know if you are married or not, or have a lady in your life.'

'You do,' he said quietly.

'I don't.'

He met her wide eyes full on. 'I wouldn't have kissed you tonight if I were romantically involved with someone else.'

Christie shrugged away the reminder of that. 'But men do. Married men have affairs——'

'So do married women.'

'Yes, true, but——'

'But what?'

'But nothing. I just suppose that those who do are a certain type.'

'Are you that certain type?'

'I'm not married, and if I were I wouldn't dream of cheating on my husband. I wouldn't want to.'

'And yet——'

'Don't say it, Victor,' Christie pleaded softly, knowing the time had come to try and make him believe that she wasn't what he thought she was, a woman scorned who'd play dirty to get her lover back. 'I'm not making a play for Paul again,' she went on sincerely. 'I know I've lost and I've accepted it. I love Michelle; she's my cousin and I wouldn't do that to her.'

She thought then that on the evidence he had thrown at her time and again he wouldn't believe that. He didn't know her, had little faith in the female mind, and he had seen what he had seen. For a second she was angry with him for doubting her and for a further second or two she desperately wanted him to believe her. Then she asked herself again why it should bother her so much what he thought, and again she couldn't answer that.

They sat in silence for a while and Christie thought that he was probably weighing up that shaky evidence and her denial to make up his mind about it. She also wondered why he was bothering. Why should it matter to him what she did or said or wanted? Unless of course it was just protection for his cousin.

'Do you believe me?' she asked at last. She wanted him to look at her and answer that, but he stared ahead, through a gap in the exotic foliage to where the sand ran into the sea, the sea into the dark horizon.

'It doesn't matter if I believe you or not,' he murmured in a throw-away fashion.

Christie's heart pulsed defensively to that. There was she, so concerned for him to think of her favourably, and really he didn't care very much what she was like. Odd, very odd, but it hurt.

'So why the grilling?' she asked quietly.

He thought about that before answering. 'I just wanted to know if your feelings for him were strong enough to do the dirty on your cousin.'

'And now I've told you I won't you still don't believe me!' His silence piled hurt on top of more hurt and she knew how to deal with it. You just walked away from it. She stood up and brushed crumbs from her skirt in a very offhand fashion. 'Well, I'll tell you something: I don't care a f . . . fig—and that is putting it politely—if you do or don't believe me! I find your interference in all this bordering on the voyeuristic. Now if you'll excuse me I'm going to get back to the party, because time spent with you gives me an uncontrollable urge to get legless!'

She turned and picked up her plate from the beach, gave him one last withering look, which was wasted because he was still studying the horizon, and stormed off down the garden path, heading for the hotel.

'Christie!' She stopped and turned because of the seriousness of his tone. He hadn't moved from the bench, just turned his head slightly in her direction. 'Be careful,' he warned darkly. 'Remember what I said about paradise and the heat and the sun.'

'How can I ever forget when you take every opportunity to slam it home to me?' Her free hand came
up and she wagged a finger at him. 'Take heed of
your own warnings, Victor Lascelles, because you are
beginning to sound as if paradise has affected you
more than anyone else!'

She strode off without another backward glance at
him. The nerve of the pious creep. Who the hell did
he think he was?

A waiter took her plate as she walked across the
terrace to the bar. The band was playing a soft,
smoochy number and couples were dancing intimately in the moonlight. A sickening loneliness hit
Christie then. Everyone had a partner but her. She
ordered a soft drink from the bar. Men like Victor
Lascelles didn't urge her into alcoholism, though a
good stiff drink might urge sleep on her tonight. Her
mind was spinning at all that had happened, and
though her body ached with weariness she knew she
wouldn't be able to sleep.

'Lover,' a soft voice whispered in her ear, and a
forceful arm snaked around her waist from behind.
'They're playing our song. Let's dance how we used
to.'

Oh, God, she could smell the drink on his breath
and she tried to spin away, but Paul was a strong
adversary.

'No, Paul, I'm...I'm going to bed...'

'A better idea.' He laughed as if it was a joke, but
Christie was sure he meant it.

Before she could stop him he had taken the drink
from her hand and whirled her on to the terrace and
taken her firmly in his arms. She didn't struggle or

protest any more because people were watching—
friends of Paul, who were laughing and having fun.

And perhaps they would see this as fun too, the
bridegroom dancing with the maid of honour to be.
And perhaps they wouldn't notice that she didn't want
this because now she could see how dangerous it all
was.

Paul held her tenderly but firmly and the music was
so soft and seductive that it was almost natural for
him to bury his mouth in her hair. The one terrible
thought that dominated all others was that Victor
Lascelles might witness this. It wouldn't be hard to
imagine the interpretation he would put on it: another
of her attempts to win back the love of the man she
had once known and loved.

Her dark eyes darted around the terrace, but there
was no sign of the lawyer, and temporarily Christie
relaxed. She could handle Paul, she was sure of that.
She couldn't have handled Victor's derision, though,
and she was unsure of that. Why should she feel so
sensitive about what he thought of her?

'We have to talk, Christie,' Paul murmured in her
ear, his arms tightening around her, his hard body
pressed so close to hers that there wasn't a whisper
of air between them. 'Let's get away from here. Let's
go down to the shore, take a romantic stroll——'

'Don't be silly, Paul,' she whispered, terrified
someone would overhear. Her eyes darted again, this
time searching for Michelle. Oh, hell, where was she?
Surely not still sleeping it off? And where was Victor
Lascelles when she needed him? Why wasn't he here?
She could put aside what he thought of her for the
benefit of what he could do for her now. If he was

here he would surely whisk her away, simply for the sake of his cousin, not for her, though the benefit would be hers alone, because now she was beginning to see what he meant. His warnings had been dished out to her, but they had been so wrongly directed. He should have warned Paul, not her, about the fearful consequences of what the heat and the sun could do to the heart.

'Am I doing the right thing, Christie?' Paul bleated in her ear. 'We had so much going for us, you and I. Is it possible to love two women at the same time? We ... we left so much unsaid, Christie, darling ...'

'Don't, Paul,' Christie pleaded, trying to strain away from him. Her whole body was aflame suddenly, not with desire but a fearful revulsion for what he was saying.

He held on to her, slowly and seductively moving her round and round till they were merely gyrating on the same spot.

'I need to talk to you, Christie, I need you to make it all right. I'm so confused. I wasn't till you turned up, but now ... now I don't know which way to turn.'

'Paul, don't talk this way. You don't know what you're saying——'

'But I do, darling. Holding you like this ... the feeling of loss ... the feeling of what might have been ...'

Christie summoned her inner reserves and pushed him back from her. She was angry now, furious with him for using her this way. In a blinding flash of wisdom she saw what she should have seen a long time ago—that Paul hadn't cared for her then and certainly didn't now and probably didn't care for

Michelle if he was doing this to her when her back was turned. For six months this man had dominated her thoughts. For six months she had undermined herself, thinking she was incapable of handling a relationship again because of him. And now she knew the true Paul, and he hadn't been worth the anguish.

But suddenly her anger evaporated on the wings of a soft Caribbean breeze, and her heart let go. Paul couldn't help this. He had had too much to drink; this perpetual partying was taking its toll on him. He wouldn't be thinking this way and saying these things if he were back in England, planning his wedding in the country of his birth. Victor was right: this was an alien world where emotions could somersault and deceive. Paul didn't love her as he had suggested. He loved Michelle and was simply suffering pre-wedding nerves.

'Paul, tomorrow we'll talk, but not tonight. Tomorrow Michelle will be her old bubbly self....'

Paul's eyes narrowed and darkened and Christie felt real fear thread through her then. She knew she had to get away before he made a scene, a scene she felt sure he would bitterly regret the next morning when he'd had time to think about it.

'I'm...I'm going to get a drink,' she told him quietly but firmly, squeezing his upper arms to reassure him that this wasn't a rejection. She didn't want to hurt him, she didn't want a scene, she just wanted to quietly slip away before he realised what was going on.

The tempo suddenly changed to a more upbeat number and suddenly there was laughter all around them. Someone called out to Paul and he turned, after giving her a bleak little-boy-lost look that tore at her heart.

She saw her opportunity to escape and escape she did, tearing herself out of his arms and dashing away towards the gardens that led to her suite.

She had hoped that Paul was so bemused with drink that he wouldn't notice which directions she took, but when she heard footsteps behind her she speeded her pace till she was almost running. She stumbled and jarred her arm against a spiky yucca, and swallowed the small cry of pain. Clutching her arm, she darted into a clump of bushes and crouched down. A giggling couple passed her on the path—Simon and Janine, friends of Paul's from London.

Her relief came out in a rush of air from her lungs and then cool common sense steadied her. Paul wouldn't come after her; he didn't need her that badly. Pushing her hair back from her damp face, she rejoined the path to her suite, her thoughts spinning so wildly in her head that she couldn't think straight.

Now she understood so much of what Victor had warned her about that she felt compelled to confide in him. She felt compelled to ask his advice too. What on earth was she going to do if Paul didn't forget this evening and tomorrow he didn't let up on her?

She wanted to leave the island, but was that possible? Could she just butt out and give a reasonable excuse for her departure? She didn't want to give anything away to her cousin, but she might if she was forced to face her. Oh, God, what a terrible mess. She could see no way out of it.

She'd gone straight past her suite and found herself on Victor's small patio entrance, and somehow that was fate. Her thoughts stilled as she stood in the marble entrance and stared at the heavy wooden door. He was probably working. Should she trouble him at this late hour? But she needed to talk—to someone.

With a will of its own her hand came up and tapped lightly on the door. She stared down at her arm; it was bleeding from the yucca. She clamped her hand over the graze and turned away from the door. She couldn't go in like this...

The door swung open and Christie twisted back to face Victor.

'I'm...I'm sorry. It...it doesn't matter...' Suddenly she was unsure again as she stared at him in the frame of the doorway. She was making a fuss about nothing, and he would think so. 'I shouldn't have...'

Her voice suddenly seized in her throat and her heart froze and her whole body shrank away from him as her wide eyes swept past Victor Lascelles to a sudden movement in the suite beyond. A flash of saffron silk, a swirl of red-gold hair... disappeared into the bedroom.

Christie stepped back in shock and stared incomprehensibly at Victor's stricken features. It was all there to see—the guilt, the dismay, the horror at being caught out. And she *had* caught them out, for, if not, why the sudden disappearance of Michelle, if they had nothing to hide? She couldn't believe this was happening, could never have envisaged all this twenty-four hours ago.

Victor stepped towards her, pulling the door shut behind him. His hand snaked out to grip her wrist to stop her escaping and held it tightly, almost fiercely.

'Oh, no, you don't!' he grated as she wrenched at him to free herself.

'Oh, yes, I do,' Christie panted angrily and with one last wrench she was free and down the steps, almost stumbling back into the shrubbery. She steadied herself and glared back at him from the path that connected all the other private suites.

'I saw what I saw and I know what I know!' she hit back at him in a screeched whisper. 'How dared you patronise me? How...how dared you dish out those warnings to me...accuse me...accuse *me* of wanting...?' Her voice went, strangled out of her throat by what she had seen. He wasn't worth wasting good breath on, this...this despicable man who was...oh, God, he was having an affair with Michelle!

Sickened, she clenched her fists to her side, furious thoughts scavenging around in her head till she thought it would burst. But one thought soared high above any others and hung suspended in the balmy night air over her head: the thought that she cared that he was involved with her cousin, and the reason she cared.

Her hand flew to her mouth and she turned and fled, though there wasn't far to flee, just next door to her not so private suite. She fumbled with the doorknob, flung open the door, and slammed it shut, falling back against it, her breath coming in ragged, pained gasps, as if they were her last.

She stood there in the darkness for a long time, drawing down that soaring thought till she held it firmly in her grasp. Michelle, though she cared deeply for her, wasn't a part of the thought, nor Paul, whom she had thought she cared deeply for but now knew she didn't. No, the thought that pulsed through her was one so absurd that she nearly tossed it back to the heavens. That flashing sight of Michelle in Victor's suite had roused a feeling she had never experienced before, not even when Michelle and Paul had announced their engagement. Jealousy wasn't an emotion she knew much about, but she suspected she had had her first experience of it.

Shakily she stepped across the spacious sitting-room and stood by the open doors, breathing the sweet night-scented air. She had rushed to Victor for his advice. He was the sort of man you would turn to in times of doubt. But had there been more to it than that?

Christie shook her head in dismay. Much more, because when she had seen that flash of Michelle she had felt a burning intensity inside her that could only be described as jealousy. She had expected him to be alone; she had wanted him to be alone. She had wanted to talk to him, to clear the air between them, to convince him she wasn't interested in Paul any more and to ask for his advice... and... and perhaps to get to know him a little better. And... and why? She wasn't prepared to analyse that yet; no, not yet, because it was all so... so preposterous. She couldn't be interested in Victor Lascelles. She wasn't so flippant with her feelings, she just wasn't!

CHAPTER FOUR

CHRISTIE spun from the bathroom basin, where she was bathing her scratched arm.

'What have you done?' Victor asked quietly from the open doorway.

Her eyes narrowed at him. 'How did you get in?' Her voice was as raw as the scratch on her arm.

'Your door wasn't locked. Careless of you. And I didn't bother to knock because I knew you wouldn't answer.'

'You can be quite astute at times, but thick-skinned in other ways,' she retorted, and gave her attention back to her arm, which was stinging like mad. 'I don't want you here in my suite and please don't think I expect an explanation. I don't.'

'But you do,' he said with authority, stepping forward into the bathroom and taking her arm to examine it as if it were his latest brief.

His touch was surprisingly warm and sensitive and Christie knew that the burning sensation she had felt in her middle when she had seen that flash of Michelle diving into his bedroom had been genuine. She studied the side of his face as he picked up a ball of cotton wool and dabbed gently at the small abrasion which was causing such a fuss. It was a good profile, strong and masculine, and yet his touch was gentle and caring. But he was a cheater, not dissimilar to Paul, and she wondered what was wrong with her for being attracted to that type of man. What the hell was the matter with her? One minute her heart was proclaiming her love for one man, then dashing it so swiftly when things had turned sour, and the next minute she was feeling so desperately shocked at the realisation that she was attracted to another. Life wasn't getting any easier; it was getting more complicated, more riddled with doubts and uncertainties.

'Nasty,' he murmured as he bent closer to make sure he had cleaned the abrasion properly. 'Shark bite?'

There was a tinge of humour in that, but Christie wasn't amused, only slightly taken aback that he could offer humour at a time like this. But he was probably trying to use wit to wriggle his way out of the embarrassing situation she had caught him in.

'Yucca,' she volunteered, stiffening away from him. 'Thanks for the first aid, though it was unnecessary. I'm quite able to tend my own wounds.'

'And bleeding hearts?' he asked as he rinsed his hands under the running tap.

'I don't suffer from a bleeding heart, not any more.'

'Oh, that sounds interesting.' He reached for a towel and rubbed his hands vigorously while watching her with those dark hooded eyes of his. When she offered nothing more he added, 'Has something happened tonight to change your heart?'

She wondered if he'd guessed what had happened between her and Paul and thought he probably had foreseen something like this coming. There must be something radically wrong with Paul's and Michelle's relationship for Paul to be making passes at her and for Michelle to be intimately involved with Victor, and with the wedding only days away.

'I have my feelings under control now,' she told him sensibly and drew a steadying breath. The bathroom was far too small and intimate an enclosure to be discussing affairs of the heart with this man. She moved out of the close area and into the bedroom beyond and through to the spacious sitting-area, where she could breathe normally.

Victor followed and they stood awkwardly facing each other, the gentle whirr of the air-conditioning the only sound.

'Is that what you came to tell me? That you had finally come to your senses and decided against pursuing your ex-lover?' he asked softly.

Christie steeled herself to stop biting back at that, but the reserve lasted only a few seconds. She crossed the room to snap off the air-conditioning, which was now playing on her nerves, adding to her misery.

She swung back to face him, sweeping her hair from her face as it settled. 'I think in the circumstances that is rather a crass thing to suggest. People in glass houses, et cetera.' She gave him a deep, meaningful look that conveyed her distaste.

'You think I am romantically involved with Michelle?' His voice was as dark as his eyes.

She stayed mute because she didn't know what to say or how to handle this. She definitely didn't want a stand-up row with him over something that was nothing to do with her. Much as she loved Michelle, she couldn't interfere. If her cousin was turning her affections to Victor that was her affair. She was tempted to try and warn Victor off her, though, but that would be useless. He wasn't the sort to listen, and she could imagine that *if* he set his sights on a woman the devil himself wouldn't be able to stop him.

He strode across the room to the bar and Christie was about to protest when she realised she didn't want to. None of this was any of her business, but there was a forever female part of her that screamed out to know it all. If he had an excuse for his despicable behaviour she *did* want to hear it. He poured two cold drinks, which indicated that he wanted to offer some explanation, and that intrigued her more. Why should he want to do that? Of course, to shut her up; that was why.

She slumped down on a sofa and watched him as he topped the drinks up with crushed ice. He placed hers on the side-table under the lamp and sat across from her.

'I'm sorry you saw what you saw——'

'Huh, sorry. The only thing you're sorry for is your own neck.'

He looked at her darkly. 'I know it probably looks that way, but——'

'It looks very much that way, Victor,' Christie interrupted yet again. 'I'm surprised you're even making an attempt to deny it after all the accusations you've dished out to me. You were quite adamant about what you thought Paul and I were up to yesterday afternoon in my suite, quite adamant. Well, I'm quite adamant in what I thought you were up to with Michelle just now.'

'The difference is that I was aware of the facts——'

'You've lost me there. And what facts were those?' she asked, mystified.

'That you and Paul were once lovers, which pre-supposes that you could well be lovers once again.'

'It does nothing of the sort!' Christie brittled back. 'And I'd like to correct you on that point. We were never lovers. I don't know what exactly Paul told you and I don't want to hear it, but what I do want is to deny any sort of sexual relationship with him. Before and now,' she emphasised strongly.

'Funny you should deny that so hotly now and not before, though,' he challenged.

'There's nothing funny at all in it. Frankly I didn't care what you thought before, but now...' Christie slowed her pace, because she was coming dangerously close to exposing a deep part of her that she wasn't quite sure about herself for the moment. 'What I'm trying to say is that the ex-lover gibe is beginning to pall, if you'll excuse the pun.'

He smiled and his eyes definitely warmed, and she wondered why. Surely not her little play on words, but what else?

'I'm very glad and relieved to hear that,' he said slowly.

Christie was surprised that he actually believed her. It made her brave enough to say her next words. 'Why should you be pleased to hear the truth?'

He studied her intently before replying slowly. 'It rather clears the dross from your past to pave the way for our future relationship.'

'Oh,' she uttered weakly, again surprised and quite disturbed by that. 'And...and what does that mean?'

'It means that I'd like to get to know you better and I don't like complications in my personal life. My work feeds me enough intrigue and indiscretions. My love-life I insist on being straight and honest——'

'You... your love-life!' Christie spluttered, not knowing whether to laugh or cry protest to that. 'I'm not part of your love-life!'

'You could very well be,' he replied coolly, almost matter-of-factly.

Christie wished she hadn't switched off the air-conditioning; heat was piling on heat here.

She forced a splutter of a laugh to her lips. 'You're something else, you know, quite something else. It takes two to have a love-life; so far you have only engaged your own dear self. I'd say you are in for a frustrating one-sided time of it.'

'Ah, so you are denying a certain attraction for me?'

Though it was stated as a question it was spoken with the authority of someone who knew the truth anyway, so what was the point of denying it? Except she would, in a way. Her laughter was genuine and unstilted now and she expected some sort of derision for her put-down, but something she knew about Victor Lascelles was that he wasn't easily put down.

She shook her head, dismissing the mirth. This was some sort of wind-up to get himself out of a tricky situation. She didn't suffer fools gladly either.

'There isn't an answer to that,' she told him, reaching for her drink and cradling it in her hands in her lap. 'I like my love-life straight and honest too, and involvement with you would be the very opposite, I suspect—bent and very dishonest. You're suggesting the impossible, because I don't fool around with men who entertain brides-to-be in their very private suite in the dead of night.'

'One particular bride-to-be,' he corrected, swallowing the last of his drink. 'And the time of night is of no importance.'

'One bride-to-be is enough, Victor, more than enough, and, as you say, the time is of no importance. You can do it mid-afternoon, mid-morning, whenever the mood takes you,' she told him flippantly.

'I'm a reserved last-thing-at-night person myself. It gives a good night's sleep, apart from all else.' He was matching her mockery and enjoying it too, far more than she was, because the thought of making love with him last thing at night—or any other time, come to that—was a very unsettling thought. 'But I gave you a fair enough hearing,' he went on. 'The least you can do is give me likewise.'

'You have given me hell since first we met, so why should I give you a fair hearing?'

'Because in spite of your flippant attitude to all this you are positively aching to know if I made it with Michelle tonight.'

She eyed him coldly across the dimly lit room. 'If I'm curious it isn't concern for what you do with your reserved personage. More a deep, sickening disgust for accusing me of doing what you are doing with the other half of the bridal pair. I saw what I saw, Victor— my cousin fleeing, no doubt with a guilty conscience, into your bedroom.'

'Hasn't it occurred to you that if what you believe were true she would be fleeing *out* of the bedroom instead of into it?'

No, it hadn't occurred to her at all, but she wouldn't admit it. Christie raised a sardonic brow. 'You claim to be a reserved person, but you might have tendencies towards a bit of perversion on the sofa or over the coffee-table,' she suggested wryly.

He threw his head back and roared with laughter. 'I can't win, can I?'

She studied him and then said quietly, 'No, I don't suppose you ever can with me.'

'But I would like to,' he said, still smiling, still amused. 'I would very much like to win with you, because as an adversary you are a tricky lady.'

'You far outsmart me, Victor,' she conceded tightly.

'I don't aim to, I assure you. I'd much rather battle it out in a more sensuous way.'

'And the sensuous way being what you like to do last thing at night, sandwiched between the cocoa and lights out?' With cynicism she matched his mocking attitude. 'Are you a lights on, *unreserved* sort of person where that is concerned?'

'That's for you to find out,' he suggested, not without a glint of humour in his dark eyes.

'That's one of life's little mysteries, along with the personal stereo and not so private suites, which shall ever remain a mystery.'

He shook his head. 'I think not, Christie, sweetheart. I think you and I are going places.'

'Do you, now? How very wrong can you get? This is one case I think you might lose.'

'Ah, but I never lose, and when I said you and I are going places I did mean that literally.'

'Oh, really? Now that sounds very mysterious,' she drawled sarcastically.

'Not at all. If you can be serious long enough I'd like to explain.'

'What, that Michelle in your suite was entirely innocent?' Christie shook her head with grim disbelief. 'You can't smooth-talk your way out of that one, Victor. There's nothing wrong with my eyesight——'

'Yes, you saw what you saw——'

'Indeed I did: Michelle frantic not to be seen by whoever tapped on your door this evening.'

'Understandable, considering the intimate nature of the reason for the visit——'

'Exactly!' she blurted triumphantly.

'Exactly nothing, Christie. You presume too much.'

'Well, we have one thing in common at the very least—a short rope of credibility. You believed Paul and I were up to no good this afternoon in my suite. I believe you and Michelle were up to no good this evening in your suite. What evil minds the pair of us harbour.'

'Another reason for us going places. Things are getting a bit hot around here, and if we think the way we do others will too.' Suddenly he stood up, over six feet of muscled deviousness. 'I think a cooling-off period for us both is in order. I doubt if either of us will be missed for a few days. Pack enough not to go without, a change or two of clothes and all the things you ladies like to clutter your dressing-tables with.'

Suddenly Christie was on her feet too, though not so steadily and determinedly as he. She was hot and confused by this sudden suggestion and furious at his chauvinistic attitude to women in general. Cluttered dressing-tables indeed!

'What on earth are you going on about?' she blurted wildly.

He looked at her as if she should know, but she didn't, of course, because he always seemed to have an edge on her in the perception stakes. 'We are going on an extended boat ride, you and I, Christie, far from the crowd, where we can get to know and hopefully enjoy each other. I have a friend with a secret hideaway on a secret island out of harm's way——'

'Just a minute,' Christie protested in astonishment. 'I'm not going anywhere with you——'

His low, low voice interjected smoothly, 'But you are, Christie, because I insist on it. If we both stay here there is going to be trouble, and I don't court trouble if I can avoid it.'

'The trouble being your involvement with Michelle, I suppose.' She didn't hide the contempt in her voice. What a rat, scuttling the burning ship when it was getting too hot for comfort.

He eyed her steadfastly, the darkness of his eyes seeming to burrow into her very soul. The temptation to concede and go with him was on the very brink of her sensible reasoning. She had even considered flight herself on the strength of what had happened between her and Paul this evening, but she didn't want to be whisked away by Victor, because his reasons for escape were so very different. He had gone too far with Michelle and was in fear of the wrath of his cousin, Paul. She didn't admire him for that. It disappointingly exposed a streak of yellow in him, apart from anything else.

'That is partly the reason,' he admitted quietly, 'but I can also see the danger for you if you stay.' He came towards her and stopped in front of her, taking her gently by the shoulders. 'I think I know why you came to me tonight. Was Paul giving you trouble?' He spoke so quietly and with such concern that all the fight drained out of her. She lowered her thick, silky lashes and stared stoically at the front of his silk shirt. A small nod was all she could answer him with.

'I thought so,' he murmured.

She shook her head slightly and then braved herself to look up and meet his eyes. 'How could you know?' she breathed softly. 'You thought I was the one doing the chasing.'

'I did at first,' he admitted. 'Now I know you a little better, and I do have an advantage over you. My work gives me insight to a lot of marital troubles. I can see the danger signals before most others.'

'W-what danger signals, and who are we talking about here?'

His hands on her shoulders slid down to her bare upper arms. 'It's late and it could take most of the night to explain, and I think an early start in the morning would be advantageous.'

Christie steeled under his gentle grasp and he let his hands slide from her. It gave Christie the opportunity to step back from him. Her strength returned, and her fight, and she wasn't going to be bamboozled off this island on such a feeble pretence.

'I'm going to stay,' she told him. 'I'm not running away from anything, because I have nothing to run away from. I can handle Paul. In the morning he will probably forget it all anyway.' Her eyes hardened. 'But I won't forget about you and Michelle——'

'No, I don't suppose you will, but it makes me wonder who your deep concern is for—your cousin or yourself.'

Christie was quick on the uptake on this one. 'Meaning you think I'm interested in you for myself? Some ego you nurture,' she breathed bitterly.

He gave a shrug, as if it mattered little to him anyway what she thought of him. 'As for Paul forgetting what happened this evening, I doubt he will,' he suggested solemnly.

'What...what do you mean?' Slowly the blood drained from her face as a very disturbing new thought began to throb inside her. Her eyes widened pleadingly. 'Mi-Michelle...she...she doesn't think...?' Oh, God, did she know Paul had made a pass at her? Had she seen something? Had Paul hinted at something?

Christie turned away from Victor and clasped her arms around herself. 'I couldn't possibly go away with you,' she said firmly. 'Michelle needs me to reassure her that there is nothing going on.'

'Michelle needs you around at the moment as badly as she needs a hole in her pretty little head.' His voice dripped contempt.

She swung back to him furiously, half fired by her own sickening guilt for what Michelle might be thinking of her. 'And no one needs you around *ever*!' she said viciously. '*Your* presence here on this paradise island of romance is as badly needed as a Swedish sauna in the desert. You're out of place and out of order and if you had any decency in you whatsoever you'd take the first flight out of here and hopefully disappear in the Bermuda Triangle on your way out.

And, talking of way out, you know where the door is! Go for it!'

She gave him the full force of her fury with the blaze of her eyes to help her vitriol on its way. God, he was like a reinforced brick wall. His eyes didn't change; his whole demeanour was as cool as an iceberg and ten times more unyielding. She couldn't get to him, one way or the other.

'I'm going, Christie Vaughan. I'm going to pack, and don't think I'm taking up your vicious advice. I value my own worth more than you obviously value yours. I'm beginning to see the thickness of *your* skin and the selfishness that powers you. You have no concern for your cousin, just a selfish disregard for other people's feelings. You want your lover back——'

'He was never my lover!' Christie almost screamed.

'And that gets to you, doesn't it? The fact that you lost out. And now you are making a last sickening effort to win——'

'Everything that comes out of your mouth is a contradiction of what you have said previously,' she interrupted heatedly. 'Minutes ago you believed me——'

'Minutes ago I didn't know you as well as I know you now. After all that has happened tonight you still want to stick around, causing more unrest. What exactly do you want, Christie?'

Christie tensed her very being till it was dangerously close to self-destruction. Now she did know what she wanted, but it didn't help. She did want escape, from everything and everyone. If she stayed, Paul might persist ... She couldn't bear the thought of it.

But how could that escape be achieved without dragging all this out into the open?

'I'm going,' she said resolutely, her mind made up in a flash. 'But not with you. I'm going solo, first thing in the morning——'

'Without any explanations?' he challenged darkly. 'Not a very nice thing to do to your cousin and mine.'

'Well, according to you, I'm not a very nice person!' she retorted, but his words hit home. She was here to give support to her cousin, to act as maid of honour at her wedding, and to run without giving a reason why was unthinkable, and to give the reason even more unthinkable. But, dear God, was there going to be any wedding the way things were going? Confusion reigned again and her head swam with it all. It was all so complicated that she couldn't think rationally any more.

'I've offered you the easy solution to all this, but you seem hell-bent on disrupting everyone's lives for your own selfish reasons,' he told her brutally. 'Stay and you'll have Paul panting around you like a rutting stag——'

'Don't be so damned disgusting! I can cope with Paul!' she bit back, quite sure she could now. She would just avoid everyone, keep out of everyone's way...but it wasn't as easy as that. This was an island and there was no true escape. And avoidance wasn't the answer anyway. Oh, God, she didn't know what to do for the best.

The brutality drained out of him and he stepped towards her and took her by her upper arms. 'Listen, Christie. I don't think in your confused state you can cope with very much at the moment and I'm offering you a way out of this uncomfortable situation.'

Christie stilled the confusion inside her and made an attempt to listen without interrupting and screaming abuse at him. The gentleness of his touch helped, as did the softening of his tone now. She nodded her head in compliance, because she needed his guidance, badly.

'As I told you, I have a friend with a holiday retreat on a nearby island . . .' Christie's eyes widened in anticipation. 'We can both escape there for a few days till things calm down here. It's another six days to the wedding and by the time we return things should have settled down between Michelle and Paul. We'll be back for the wedding——'

Christie couldn't contain herself any longer. 'How can there be a wedding now? They're having marital problems *before* the event,' she cried helplessly. 'Do you think——?'

'I think we can help by not being here, both of us.'

'Removing the temptation?' She breathed heavily. She was Paul's temptation and this Victor Lascelles was at least making an effort to stop his affair with Michelle, which was something, she supposed. But there was still an ocean of doubts to be resolved. 'How...how can we do that? Just disappear and then reappear for the wedding as if nothing has happened? It's impossible. We'll be making it all ten times worse.'

'We'll be doing nothing of the kind,' Victor said quietly. 'Remember what I said about paradise——'

'Oh, not that again,' Christie breathed mournfully and pulled away from him. She stood by the patio doors with her back to him and her arms clutched around her. She hated paradise. It deceived and twisted emotions till you were spinning with confusion.

'Everyone here is running on a high, Christie,' he murmured behind her. 'We can make that paradise work for us. No one will think anything of the best man and the maid of honour going off together for a few days as lovers.'

'Lovers?' she exploded and swung back to face him. He was standing so close that when she swung she was nearly in his arms. He was smiling mysteriously at her and in that second she felt his fearful magnetism and almost longed for them to be that way. But it was only a fleeting longing, a snap of idiocy that rocked her insides. Reality was only a flash away, though, the reality of Michelle in his suite, up to no good.

'That's what people will think,' he told her softly. 'And it's the only logical excuse for our disappearance. We've been seen together often enough——'

'We never have!' Christie protested.

'Don't you believe it. We have adjoining suites, we've had breakfast together, we were at the buffet together, we sat in the gardens to eat together——'

'But no one saw us!' Christie interjected, shaking her head. But possibly someone had. 'And...and even if they had it's not enough, not nearly enough,' she added weakly.

'I promise you it is.' His eyes almost convinced her that it was. 'But if you want to make it failsafe we can easily take a moonlight stroll along the beach now.

Most people are still dancing on the terrace, and we'd be seen.'

Christie let out a snort of incredulous laughter. 'You're really serious, aren't you?'

'I'm very serious about our getting off this island for a while.' His eyes held hers, seriously. The tone of his voice emphasised that seriousness. He *was* serious!

Christie gazed at him in astonishment and her voice came out in a besieged croak. 'You want people to believe we are lovers?'

He was smiling again, that very charismatic smile that had her insides all confused and disruptive again. She was oh, so tempted. She did need escape and so did he, and together they might achieve it, no questions asked.

'It...it seems a bit...a bit extreme,' she murmured weakly. She shook her head, uncertain, confused. 'No...it wouldn't be right.'

'It wouldn't be right to stay in the circumstances,' he persuaded softly.

Her circumstances, his circumstances. To be logical about it all, it was the decent thing to do. If she stayed, Paul might... If Victor stayed, it could destroy Paul's and Michelle's relationship...

'I...I don't know...'

'I do. Trust me.' He clasped her hand tightly and before she had a chance to murmur another protest he hauled her out on to the patio and down the steps past the whirlpool, towards the gate that led directly on to the beach.

But she didn't trust him, not an inch, not after seeing Michelle in his suite. But so what if she didn't trust him? At least he was offering her a way out of her dilemma. If they were seen to be romantically involved Paul would ease up on her and himself, and that would be one problem dealt with. Victor's problem he could sort out for himself. She wondered just how deeply he was involved with Michelle. Did he actually love her? Did she actually love him? If so, why on earth was she contemplating marriage to Paul and why was Victor letting her get away with it? The awful answer to that was they weren't in love, simply having a pre-wedding fling with each other. Disgust rose inside her like a fearful indigestion.

'There is absolutely no need for that!' she protested as he draped his arm suggestively around her shoulders as they strolled along the warm sand at the edge of the sea, heading towards the hotel terrace, where most of the hardy revellers were gathered, laughing and dancing into the small hours.

'There is every need if you want to do this properly,' he grated, tightening his grip and yet caressing at the same time.

But there was absolutely no need for what Victor Lascelles did when they walked far enough towards the hotel to be noticed by the wedding guests *and* Paul, who was propped up against the bar, eyeing them suspiciously.

Satisfied that they were being watched, Victor swept her into his arms, so strongly and determinedly that she had no chance but to meld helplessly against him.

The kiss was powerfully executed with all the right ingredients to make it evident to the world that this was serious. His mouth was hot and passionate and his arms so determinedly wrapped around her, claiming her body so intimately to his, that it was on the brink of censorship. It went on and on, the kiss that she endured because she had to. She willed herself not to act in kind, not to submit outwardly to the impassioned embrace, but inside she burned with a heat she had never experienced before. The fever raged inside her, her need so nearly out of control, just hanging on by a thread of decency and the thought that the desire he showed was all part of the game.

He *was* acting, so she told herself, simply putting on a show to make it all look like the genuine article, two people helplessly submitting to the magic of what the Caribbean could do to hearts. But she knew his would be as cold as stone while hers was racing erratically, doomed to no good.

His mouth released hers at last, but he was still playing the part, gazing down at her with unbridled desire in his eyes. When his hand came up to tenderly smooth away a wisp of hair from her brow to make room to press his lips sensuously against her warm skin she thought he was in the wrong profession. He should be treading the boards of Broadway, not treading the corridors of divorce courts.

Slowly he turned her back, away from the wedding guests, back towards their suites along the beach.

'Exit stage left,' she uttered drily.

'End of Act One,' he said solemnly, confirming to Christie that it had indeed been a great performance.

For a moment she had been stage-struck; now the applause inside her was fading away, leaving her feeling desolate and so deflated that she wondered what was happening to her.

'Well, don't get any ideas that Act Two will hot up, Victor Lascelles. The safety curtain is well and truly down!'

He was laughing softly in the balmy night air as once out of sight of the others she drew away from him and broke into a run, back to the safe haven of her suite. She could still hear his soft, low, mocking laughter ringing in her ears as she slammed shut her gate and ran into the sitting-room, drawing the patio doors shut behind her, shutting out him and the world and the heat of paradise which was swirling her emotions till she wasn't at all sure about anything any more.

CHAPTER FIVE

'I'VE changed my mind,' Christie told him the next morning when she answered the front door of the suite.

It was so early that she could hardly keep her eyes open. What little sleep she had managed had left her unsatisfied and fragile. She shut the door quietly after him.

He faced her. He looked as if nothing had troubled him through the night. He was clean-shaven, rested and ready to take on the world. 'It makes no difference; you're coming anyway.'

'I thought you'd say that,' she said wearily.

'So why didn't you pack?' He glanced around the room, looking for her bag.

'Just thought I'd put up a protest to the last. Can't you see any other way out of this?' she asked hopefully, tightening her robe around her. She'd spent the night considering that there must be another option open to them, but had come up with nothing that made any sense.

'I haven't given it a thought,' he stated nonchalantly. 'When I make a decision, it's made—no going back.'

His eyes raked her up and down as if that decision meant more than what they were talking about.

Christie's body pulsed beneath her thin covering of virginal white satin, and she let it, because he wasn't that smart. He'd never know how deeply he disturbed her, because what was inside her was all hers. She knew she would go with him and knew she could cope with it, because she had before. She was adept at hiding her feelings now.

Feelings? How could she have any for this man? What she knew of him wasn't very nice, but she wasn't very clever in her choice of men, though this man was no choice, just someone offering her an easy way out of a tricky situation.

'Come on, then,' he urged. 'Get packing—or shall I do it for you? I warn you, though, I'll miss something vital, for sure——'

'All right, all right. Message received.' She flounced into her bedroom and in sixty seconds had packed enough for decency. She spent another minute throwing herself into denim shorts, a cinnamon-brown camisole top and a pair of matching espadrilles, and dragging a brush through her mass of tousled dark hair.

'Done,' she said flatly as she dumped the holdall at his feet.

He smiled in admiration and then promptly turned towards the door without picking up the bag. 'That's what I like, a woman who acts like a man,' he grated over his shoulder.

'Chauvinist bleep!' she uttered under her breath as she picked up the bag and followed him out of the door.

She noted his laptop computer next to her in the back of the taxi as it sped them towards a marina. She was slightly consoled by its presence. He intended to work for the duration; well, so would she. She had notes to prepare for some future interviews. The days with him would speed by and then they would return . . . Despondency descended like the thick buff clouds that were accumulating on the Caribbean horizon. What would they find when they returned to the wedding island? Victor's blue bird of happiness squawking its lungs out on the threshold of a marriage that really shouldn't be taking place?

'I wish I hadn't come,' Christie told him as he helped her on to the deck of a small motor cruiser he had hired to take them to his friend's island.

'Too late now,' he said, tight-lipped, as he tossed their bags down beside her. 'It's for the best,' he added.

'I don't mean this trip,' she told him, helping him to unwind the ropes that secured them to the quayside. 'I just wish I hadn't come to this wedding at all. I mean, none of this would have happened . . . well, none of this with Paul. You're something else, having an affair with the bride-to-be. If you hadn't come and I hadn't come——'

'Will you shut up, Christie?' His voice was strained. 'You don't know anything about boats by any chance, do you?' He looked, boot-faced, at the instrument panel, as if it was the first one he had ever seen.

Christie paled and leapt to her feet from the seat in the blunt end of the cruiser, where she had been slumped in defeat.

'Are you crazy?' she spluttered. 'Don't you know how to drive this thing?'

'I think you pilot a boat, not drive it, but I could be wrong.'

'I'm off!' Christie screeched, lunging for her bag. The man was a madman!

Suddenly the engine burst into life and they shot away from the quayside with such a fierce thrust that she was thrown back in to the rear seat. Christie gripped the armrests so fiercely that her knuckles whitened instantly.

Minutes later she had to admit that Victor Lascelles was as quick to pick up the intricacies of seamanship as he was at the lambada. The boat settled and was soon cleaving through the crystal water like a gleaming dolphin.

Christie relaxed as much as she was able in the circumstances and watched the muscles of his back bunching under his white T-shirt as he changed course, swinging the boat to circle a swirl of turbulence in the water. The man intrigued her. He wasn't easy to understand. He seemed to have such a cynical attitude to marriage, but she supposed what he did for a living made him that way. Perhaps by the end of this trip she might know him a bit better, but did she honestly want to? She still hadn't got over the shock of finding Michelle in his suite last night, a double-edged shock for realising he was illicitly involved with her and for realising she cared for her own sake along with Michelle's. How could she be attracted to a rat like that? His paradise theory loomed large, and for once she had to agree that it held water. It really did do strange things to the emotions. Those kisses of his and the effect they'd had on her was prove of that.

An hour later they reached their destination, a true Robinson Crusoe island that took Christie's breath away. They had left behind the swollen storm clouds off the coast of Grenada and the sky was now clear, the sun white-hot overhead, glancing off the glaring white beaches and brilliant green foliage that rose up into a hillock in the centre of the island.

It was a tiny island, a snatch of white and green paradise plopped into a pale aquamarine pool of sea. No sign of life. No sprawling villa at the end of the sun-bleached wooden jetty Victor was leaping on to after cutting the engine and letting the boat drift lazily towards it.

Christie tossed the bags on to the wooden platform as he tied up, gingerly propped his computer against them, and ignored his outstretched hand to help her ashore.

'I can't see any sign of civilisation,' she remarked as she leapt from the boat, her head aching from the sun beating down on it, and the wind thrashing her hair into a tangled mass.

'The house is well hidden,' he told her, reaching for their bags. Christie helped by picking up his computer.

'Are you sure your friend won't mind us just turning up like this?'

'She isn't here.'

He led the way along the jetty, down on to the hot beach towards a path that cut through the fertile undergrowth.

'She? Your mother? A girlfriend? An ex-wife? The cat's mother?'

'A grateful client,' he muttered, but offered no more.

How grateful? Christie wondered as she dragged her feet after him. More than borrow-my-house-any-time grateful?

That conjecture was swept aside at the sight of the lovely wooden house approached from a leafy walkway just a stone's throw from the white beach. The contrast between the glaring brilliance of white sand, pale blue sea and sky and the coolness of the dark wood secret house tucked in among dense green foliage was stunning and a very welcome relief.

Christie flopped into a rattan chair on the shady veranda while Victor searched a pocket of his holdall for keys. The view from the veranda was breath-taking, down the leafy walkway to the beach and the sea curling gently over the sand. There was noise, plenty of it, blissful tropical sounds of exotic birds and chirruping tree frogs, sea swishing on sand, palm trees stirring in the warm breeze.

'This *is* paradise, isn't it?' he said behind her, his hands gripping the back of her seat and following her gaze down to the beach.

'Utopia,' Christie breathed. It suddenly struck her that they appeared to be completely alone in this dangerous Utopia. 'Is ... are we alone here? I mean are there any other houses around?' She swivelled her head to look up at him.

'None.'

'Oh,' Christie murmured. She got to her feet, just a little perturbed by that but it was controllable. All she had to do was remind herself of the caution she had vowed.

'It could be difficult for us both——'

'Not at all,' she said hastily, reaching down to pick up her bag. 'So long as we both are mature about this I see no problems. We can share a house without getting involved with each other——'

His laugh cut her off mid-sentence. 'I meant it could be difficult managing on canned food and dry goods while we're here, apart from these of course.' To her astonishment he squatted down and took out of his leather holdall a huge iceberg lettuce, a bag of tomatoes and several fat christophene marrows. 'Do you think we can stretch these over four days?'

Christie was speechless. Her mouth gaped open. Victor grinned up at her. 'I foraged for these in the hotel kitchen.'

Christie found her voice. 'You stole them?' she suggested, aghast that he could do such a thing.

'Of course not. The hotel was happy to oblige.' He stood up. 'Come inside, I'll show you around.'

'Just a minute. Is . . . is that all we've got to eat? I mean there can't be any electricity here, no fridge, no shops——'

'Bottled gas fridge and Delia always keeps a stock of unperishables here. I hope you are a fish person, because——'

'Fish? Not that awful dried saltfish stuff . . .'

'No, not that awful dried saltfish stuff,' he told her on sufferance. 'If it's escaped your notice, we are surrounded by a living larder here. We'll fish every day and barbecue on the beach and generally get back to nature.' He grinned at her open-mouthed look of amazement. 'Come on, Christie, where's your sense of adventure?'

It occurred to her that Victor was quite delighted to be here. Yes, he was a solitary man and this idyllic isolation appealed to him. She understood that somehow, but she wasn't going to agree with him.

'I don't have one,' she mumbled as she tightened her grip on her bag and followed him into the lovely wooden house. 'I'm strictly a fast-food freak; a local hamburger take-away on the doorstep is as far as my sense of adventure takes me,' she added as she stopped in the middle of the main room of the house. 'Oh, this is lovely,' she breathed in relief, letting her bag drop to the polished wooden floor. She hadn't really known what to expect, but this was beyond her dreams.

There was just enough light through the open door to see. The room was very simply furnished with cool rattan sofas covered in blue and ecru ethnic cloth; the mahogany beeswaxed floors were scattered with alabaster-white rugs with deep fringes, and because of the simplicity it was pure good taste. Bamboo tables and rush-seated stools and blue and white chinese urns gave it a colonial feel. There was timber panelling everywhere and the ceiling was high, criss-crossed with beams, giving space and a fair degree of coolness to the place now that the front door was open and a breeze from the sea swirled gently in. Singapore fans hung suspended from some of the beams.

'How do those work if there's no electricity?' she asked him as he moved about the room, throwing open the shutters at the windows to let more light and air in.

'There's a solar-powered generator somewhere,' Victor told her vaguely. 'I'll get it going later. That's your room over there.' He nodded his head across the room and went through a wide opening to a kitchen, again a surprise to Christie, as it was so well fitted out that it wouldn't have been out of place in a New York penthouse.

'This is a strange place,' she remarked as she watched him ignite the pilot light of the double-doored fridge. 'It's simple yet affluent, if you know what I mean. Funny place to find on a tiny tropical island.'

'It's Delia's retreat,' he told her, opening the doors to put in the salad he'd thoughtfully brought with them. 'She came out of her divorce punch-drunk with grief, but a very wealthy lady, thanks to me.'

'And happiness can be bought, can it?' Christie asked, slightly cynically.

Victor turned to her, his eyes as inscrutable as ever. 'No, it can't,' he said quietly and then added, 'But money can help.'

'Are you one of those divorce lawyers who, for a price, screws the neck of an ailing marriage till it squeals?'

Christie really didn't know why she'd said that. To her ears it sounded almost bitterly scathing, as if she'd been through a harrowing divorce herself, which she hadn't.

The room was suddenly very quiet, except for the plop, plop of the fridge as it got into motion.

Victor looked at her coldly. 'You seem to bear a grudge against anyone making a living in such a way.'

Christie leaned against the archway that separated the kitchen from the sitting-room. The reason for her cynicism hit her. It was this Delia, this grateful close friend of his. By the looks of her retreat she must be a beautiful lady, wealthy too. This was strange, so strange, feeling this pull in her heart chamber for a woman she didn't know and for a man she scarcely knew. It was almost a jealousy thing for Victor's close involvement with the owner of this house, a jealousy thing for what he had with Michelle, a jealousy thing she really couldn't understand but which was powering her abrasive attitude towards him.

She lowered her eyes. 'I'm sorry,' she breathed. 'I didn't mean to sound so cynical. I suppose it's because I have such high ideals about love and marriage. People get themselves into such messes when they fall in love.' She felt herself colouring. She too had got herself into a mess over Paul, so where had her high ideals been then?

'And people need help when it goes wrong,' he said and then added quietly and somehow meaningfully, 'and some people need it before it goes wrong.'

'You sound as if you'd be more suited to marriage guidance than winding up broken marriages.'

He smiled ruefully. 'And some people think, because I do what I do, I know the secret of what makes a marriage tick.'

Christie frowned in puzzlement. 'What do you mean?'

He leaned back against the fridge and crossed his arms. 'Why did you come to me last night?'

Christie shrugged. 'I suppose . . . well . . . I suppose I needed to talk.' She smiled slowly as he raised a brow. It wasn't a raised brow of disbelief, but one of knowing. 'I get what you're getting at.' She laughed softly. 'You're the sort of person people come to when they have a problem.'

'I'm afraid I am,' he murmured. 'But I don't have the secret of life and happiness, I just listen, and that's enough really. So do you want to talk about your problem with Paul?'

'There isn't one,' she told him bravely. 'Not any more. I was confused last night. Not wholly for myself.' She held his gaze intently. 'I've coped with that over the months, but it shook me up that Paul could make a pass at me last night. I know he'd had too much to drink, but sometimes when you're drunk the truth comes out. I saw Paul as someone very unstable in any sort of relationship with a woman, and it frightened me to think I could have been the one in Michelle's place, that I could have made a mistake as so many others do. He asked me if it was possible to love two women at once.' She shook her head. 'If I'd had any feelings left for him that would have finished them all off.'

'One man, one love, one woman, one love?'

Christie nodded. 'I can't see it being any other way. It *has* to be that way or the whole marriage institution is doomed. When I came to you last night I was confused, more concerned for Paul than myself, though I must admit I was confused as to how to handle him.' Her eyes widened appealingly. 'He's here in the Caribbean to be married, so what is suddenly going wrong for him?'

Suddenly she realised what she was saying. It was a silly question when the answer was facing her. Did Paul know about Michelle's and Victor's involvement with each other? She voiced the icy thought.

'Does he know about you and Michelle?'

'Know what about us?' he asked coolly.

'Well . . . well, that . . . that she was in your suite last night?' Christie felt sure that he didn't. Paul had told her what Michelle had told him—that she'd had too much sun and champagne and needed a rest. Her disappointment in Michelle was only equalled by her disappointment with everyone else concerned in this mess, including herself for running away from it.

'I shouldn't think for a minute that he did.' His voice was so level and smooth that Christie felt a spur of anger in the base of her spine.

'Do you think he has any idea what you're both up to behind his back?'

His tone didn't alter. 'I shouldn't think for a minute that he does.'

'And don't you think for a minute that he probably *does* and that was probably why he got drunk and made a pass at me?' she thrust at him.

Victor eased himself away from the fridge and drawled wearily, 'And don't try to shift the blame on to my shoulders for what Paul did to you. I don't think for a minute that he made a pass at you for any other reason than you were there for the taking.'

'Thanks!' Christie breathed furiously, trying in vain to hold her temper. 'That says a lot for me, doesn't it?'

She didn't want an answer to that so she turned abruptly, snatched up her bag, and strode purposefully across to her bedroom. She didn't even look at the room, but thudded across it to open the shutters to let in some fresh air.

'You took that the wrong way, Christie,' he said solemnly from the open doorway. 'I meant that any woman would have done.'

Christie spun, very nearly hurt by that. 'Well, thanks again. That doesn't do much for my ego either.'

'You want it all ways, don't you? As a lot of women do. You apparently didn't want Paul's attentions last night, yet you feel insulted when I tell you that any woman would have done for him. You think you know so much, but in fact you know very little.'

'I know that you are not a very nice person,' she blazed, 'and that I was incredibly stupid in coming to you last night thinking you might be able to put me straight.'

'I'm very capable of putting you straight, Christie, but I don't choose to till your attitude changes. You're not receptive enough yet for any hard reasoning. I suspect that what you really wanted to know last night was whether Paul was swinging your way and you were in with a chance with him——'

She picked up the nearest thing to hand—fortunately a cushion from a chair by the window. It didn't even leave her hand, because Victor's reactions were much quicker. He was suddenly there in front of her and snatched the cushion from her and flung it behind him. It landed with a dull thump against the wardrobe across the room.

'Temper, temper,' he cajoled so insolently that it forced more temper to her senses. She was shaking with it.

He gripped her shoulders to steady her. 'You make me so damn angry,' she blurted.

'And I suppose it has never occurred to you that you make me damn mad too?'

She felt his 'damn mad'; it bit into her shoulders. 'Because I won't accept what you *think* you are—some self-righteous, pompous lawyer whom everyone flees to in their hour of need? You'll be telling me next that

that was why Michelle was . . . was in . . . your . . . your suite . . .'

Her fury slowed and her words shunted like a steam train slowing for fear of hitting the buffers. No, not that; it couldn't be so innocent, could it? No, it damned well couldn't, because he would have said so before now, and besides, what problems could Michelle possibly have? She adored Paul. Oh, dear God, not that awful bone-gnawing thought again. *Did* Michelle think Paul was interested in her cousin again? Had she seen her cousin as a rival for the man she was going to marry and gone to Victor for advice last night?

Her whole body slackened in Victor's grip. 'I am receptive, Victor, please believe that. I want to know so much. It's driving me crazy, thinking that I might be the cause of everyone else's problems. I mean, did . . . was it my fault Michelle was with you last night? Did she turn to you because she thought there was still something between me and Paul? Was it my fault Paul made a pass at me? Was I asking for it?' She shook her head as it swam with confusion. She really didn't know what was going on, and it *was* driving her crazy.

'Tell me how you feel about Paul before I tell you anything,' he said gently.

Her eyes widened. 'Why?' she murmured, feeling his grip soften to that tantalising caress that seemed to indicate something not very nice was coming.

'Because I'm still not sure how you feel about him and I don't want to hurt you, and it might if you still cared very deeply . . .'

She shook her head again, scarcely able to look him in the eye. He helped her by lifting her chin so she had no choice but to meet his gaze. His eyes didn't penetrate so deeply now, were not half so accusing, but there was a glimmer of doubt and she wanted to clear it. She swallowed hard before speaking.

'I meant it when I said I didn't love Paul any more,' she whispered. 'I really did come to terms with it when he rejected me for Michelle. But I suppose there was a small part of me that still hung on, though that disappeared last night when he was saying all those things. I saw him differently, saw how unstable he was. Now I realise that I probably never had really loved him.' She tried to smile. 'I suppose I was just infatuated with him for a while. He was a breath of fresh air compared to most of the men I meet, so open and fun-loving. I loved his zest for life, but couldn't really match his pace. Michelle could, and that's why they're so well suited.' She sighed. 'I don't know what's going on, Victor. It's why I came to you last night. Paul frightened me and then when . . . when I saw Michelle with you I just thought . . . well, you didn't deny it . . . you still haven't denied it.'

'I didn't think I needed to,' he said quietly. 'I still don't think I need to. In fact I'll go further and say I won't deny it.' Christie went cold inside, and, as if he knew, Victor hardened his grip. 'It's beneath my contempt to deny such a thing,' he added. 'You should never have thought it of me or your cousin in the first place.'

'OK, so now you're making me feel guilty,' she replied quickly. 'But all the same you must admit it was all very suspicious, just as suspicious as Paul being in my suite for ages that afternoon. He fell asleep, as it happened; that was all that went on. He fell asleep and I left him to it. He came to my suite, I suppose to see if I was OK... but... but...'

'But maybe he didn't——'

'I don't know!' Christie suddenly blazed, then she softened her tone. 'We had a drink and then he fell asleep and I went and had a shower and when I came out he was awake and saw me wrapped in a towel and looked... looked a bit strange...'

'As if he still wanted you?'

'He never wanted me in the first place,' Christie admitted quietly. 'That was what was so weird about it all. Why now, and why say those things to me last night? And why... why did Michelle go to you, if it wasn't what I thought? Why did she dart into your bedroom like that?'

He didn't answer but seemed to be waiting for her to work it out for herself. Christie licked her very dry lips. He didn't want to help her to understand. He wanted her to work it out for herself, and she was... yes, she was.

'Did she come to you for the same reason as I did?' she whispered at last. 'For... for advice?'

'You tell me.'

'Was she... confused?'

'Go on.'

'Unsure... worried about Paul... worried... that maybe... maybe they weren't doing the right thing in... in getting married?'

Again he stayed mute and in that silence the confusion started to clear. 'It's nothing to do with us, is it? They... they *are* having doubts about this... this marriage.' Her voice was so raw that it hurt in her throat. 'Oh, dear God,' she husked, lowering her head in misery at the thought, and then her head jerked up. 'But why didn't you tell me all this?'

He released her then as if he had only been holding her till the truth dawned. 'Because it's always best to work it out for yourself, Christie. And several other reasons. If you had known you would have wanted to stay and help——'

'Of course I would!' she snapped, angry now for having been so easily whisked away from her two dear friends, who needed her now.

'And that is why I needed to get you away. Neither you nor I are any good to them at the moment, Christie. It's their lives and they need to sort out their problems for themselves. As I said before, you're a temptation, a reminder to Paul of a life when he had no responsibilities; now they're looming on the horizon and he's panicking. If you had stayed you both might have done something you would have regretted——'

'I wouldn't,' Christie protested. 'I wouldn't, Victor, I wouldn't have been tempted to do anything with Paul. You must believe that!'

'I do, Christie, now I do, I promise you, but think of Paul. All the time you were on that island you were a temptation; now it's removed. Michelle was having the same doubts, pre-wedding nerves, fearful that she too is making a mistake. It's why she came to me last night—to ask my advice.'

'But it must be a mistake if they're having doubts,' Christie reasoned. 'This wedding shouldn't take place. You don't have doubts when you're truly in love.'

'How do you know?'

The cool, calm question nearly floored Christie. Her eyes widened and she stared hopelessly at him. He stood in front of her, this cool man who seemed to have such an air of wisdom about him that he was a towering pillar of good sense. All he said was true and oh, how she understood Michelle turning to him for help.

'And...and how do you know you are right and to leave them to sort out their own problems is the right thing to do?' she argued weakly.

'I don't know, Christie,' he told her sensibly. 'I've never been in love myself, but I know myself, and I know when it does hit me I won't turn to anyone else for help if I suffer any doubts. *If* they arise I'll ask myself a few simple questions and then I'll ask the lady concerned the same questions.'

'What...what sort of questions?' Christie whispered.

'Can I live without her? Can she live without me? Do I want to spend the rest of my life with her? Does she want to spend the rest of her life with me? Can I come to terms with her playing her personal stereo too loud?'

Christie's whole body tensed till she realised he was trying to lift the weight of this discussion to a lighter plane. His eyes were warm brown, not mocking but certainly humorous. She tried a weak smile to match his levity.

'But that's the way you think is right for you; some people can't hack it on their own. Paul and Michelle need to talk to somebody. They tried and we let them down. If we'd stayed Paul and I would have worked something out. You had already made a start with Michelle. What ... what did you tell her?'

He shrugged his wide shoulders. 'I told her nothing, because where love is concerned you can't be told. First rule of marriage counselling: just listen. I've proved that with you, Christie; I let you work things out for yourself.'

'You didn't at first,' she told him ruefully. 'You made awful accusations.'

He smiled. 'Just to help you on your way, and I'm not a professional, remember. At the moment Paul and Michelle need to talk to each other and no one else. They don't need either of us, and, if it helps, I'm convinced they are right for each other. It's one reason why I wanted to know your true feelings for Paul. I didn't want to hurt you by telling you I believe he's truly in love with Michelle and no one else. She's in love with him too, but they are both experiencing pre-wedding jitters. Personally I think they have done the wrong thing in surrounding themselves with a shower of so-called friends slurping champagne morning, noon and night when they should be concentrating their feelings on each other. Marriage is a serious business.'

'And there endeth the first lesson,' Christie mocked softly.

'Don't you agree with me?'

She nodded, scooped her hair from her face, and turned to the open window. 'You know I do. I can think of nothing worse than having a crowd around me at such a precious time.'

'How would you do it, then?'

Suddenly he was behind her, slipping his arms around her waist. She didn't panic, just accepted his touch, because she had no fight left in her. This discussion and his revelations—no, not his revelations... her own realisations—had drained her. She was so fond of Paul and Michelle, but in a way she was glad she was out of it all. Victor was so right; they needed time and space on their own. There was only one tiny doubt in her demisting thoughts. She had space and time too, four days of it, but she was going to have to share them with this tower of good sense who had kissed her and said he wanted to know her better and had persuaded her to come to this remote little slice of paradise where emotions could so easily be tricked and fooled into a state of false well-being. She would have to be very sensible because, though he had the basis of common sense and knew the dangers of paradise, he wasn't so clever at heeding his own warnings.

'It rather clears the dross from your past to pave the way for our future relationship...' His words kept coming back to haunt her. The dross was gone now, her love for Paul no longer a threat because now she knew it had never been there in the first place. Victor Lascelles had seen that off. And now the way was clear for his own intentions, which he had made quite obvious with words and actions. The others back on Grenada believed them to be lovers, and he had suggested they very well could be. And how easy to slip into the role, how very easy for any woman...but she wasn't any woman. Christie Vaughan had ideals and she doubted Victor Lascelles could ever rise to them, in spite of being a very attractive man.

She drew away from him then and moved across the room to unpack her bag. He was still waiting for her answer and she at least owed him some sort of a reply. Stilling the turbulence inside her, she said quietly, 'I can't say till it happens.'

'What happens?' he asked smoothly.

She didn't dare look at him, because her nerves were jangling so, and he might hear them ringing out like church bells.

'I haven't fallen in love yet and that comes before all else.'

He laughed softly and her eyes were glued to the zip of her holdall. She heard him move to the door.

'I'm going fishing for our lunch. Do you want to come?'

It was going to be all right. Her heart only fluttered slightly at the thought that they might come out of this as friends instead of lovers.

Without lifting her eyes from the bag, she ripped the zip open. 'No, thanks. You hunt, I'll make house, Tarzan.'

He laughed again and was gone and Christie stared bleakly at the contents of her holdall. She'd forgotten her underwear, and Freud, if he were here, would fall about laughing at that.

CHAPTER SIX

CHRISTIE unpacked. The bedroom was lovely, simply but tastefully furnished, like the rest of the house. There was a small shower-room off the dressing area at the far end of the room, and Christie wondered where the water came from, but didn't succumb to the temptation of a cool shower in case the water was rationed.

In the room was a huge bamboo four-poster that rose up like a pagoda to a point, and there were cool linen sheets and pillowcases in a box at the foot of it. She made up the bed and slid open a latticework door which she thought was a cupboard, but was in fact the sliding door to the veranda that ran the length of the house. It was all so lovely... She breathed a sigh of contentment. It was the most perfect place for a honeymoon.

No, she didn't want to think about honeymoons or weddings in paradise or even her companion for the next few days. She wanted to blank off and enjoy.

Victor's room was much the same as her own. She resisted the temptation to unpack for him, though she was curious to know what he had brought to wear and to occupy himself with, but she made up his bed for him. It was the least she could do while he was out fishing for their lunch.

At the back of the kitchen she found a store-room stacked with canned goods and crates of bottled water and soft drinks *and* wine and beer. She hoped she wasn't being presumptuous by taking some of the stuff to stock the fridge with.

Hotter than ever by this time, she went outside to wander around the house, and found such an abundance of hibiscus shrubs and luxuriant ferns and sweet-scented jasmine and purple bougainvillaea that she felt no guilt at picking bunches to put on the table on the veranda and the low bamboo coffee-table in the sitting-room.

Eventually she changed into a bikini and made her way down to the beach to cool her bare feet in the warm sea and to look out for Victor. The boat was moored quite a way out to sea and she could just see the line of his rod against the horizon and a bright yellow umbrella on deck, and suspected he might be asleep under it.

She gathered driftwood for a fire later, collected a stack of shells she felt sure she would forget when they left, waded out to sea for a cooling swim, and then made her way to a shady palm and collapsed under it to fall asleep immediately.

She was awoken from a dreamless state by a very dream-like pressure on her lips—warm, soft, alluring, a definite hint of something more, even a promise maybe.

The pressure receded with the blinking open of her eyes, eyes that looked up into his warm brown eyes, which seemed to have lost all the tension and intrigue of the past.

'I've hunted; your turn now,' he whispered softly as he flopped down beside her on the warm shady sand.

Christie hitched herself up on to her elbows. 'Did you kiss me just now?'

'You bet,' he murmured, closing his eyes. He had incredible lashes, jet and silky, thick and long. His body hair was something too; dark and tightly coiled, it suggested some foreign ancestry. He wore cut-off shorts—not designer, that was for sure. Faded and worn, they too suggested a mysterious past.

'Just because you thought it a good idea to pretend we were lovers in Grenada, you don't have to take your method acting to its extremes, you know.'

'I wasn't acting then and I'm not acting now,' he breathed slowly and lazily. 'And don't protest or even argue, Christie; it's far too hot for that. Just accept that we're going to enjoy ourselves while we're here.'

'People have different ideas on enjoyment,' she drawled smoothly. 'Yours is obvious; mine is——'

'The same as mine,' he interrupted without opening his eyes.

Christie stared down at him and pulled a face, and then got to her feet, very tempted to kick sand over him as he lay so relaxed beneath the palm.

'So where is this maritime feast I've been waiting so long for...? Dear God, is that it?' She stared in horror at at least a foot and a half of plump red- and silver-scaled fish flesh lying pathetically in the sand at his feet.

'Not bad for a beginner, is it?' He sat up, clutched his knees, and gazed proudly down at his catch, as if it were his first-born.

'What the devil is it?' Christie breathed.

'Search me.'

'But...but it could be something poisonous, something unfit for human consumption,' Christie argued, delicately prodding it with the tip of her toe.

'Dolphins are practically human and you don't see many of those writhing around with stomach cramps after eating them.'

Half laughing, she spluttered, 'Don't be so flippant, Victor. And how do you know dolphins eat them?'

'Because one was in the check-out queue when I was battling for this little monster.'

'You should have let him have it,' she said scornfully.

'It's dog eat dog in the wild blue yonder, Christie. Come to think of it, it could be a dog fish——'

'A dog fish is a small shark and this hasn't got teeth...has it?' she added with a murmur, squatting down to examine it more closely. 'Tiny ones,' she observed. She sat back in the sand. 'What do we do with it?'

He grinned. 'What do *you* do with it? I caught it; you cook it.'

'No way, Pedro the fisherman,' she laughed. 'I gathered wood for the barbecue; *you* cook it!' She shot to her feet and was about to make her way back to the house when he caught her by her ankles and pulled her back down to the sand.

Turning her to him, he pulled her hard against him. If he hadn't been smiling when she looked at him she might have thought he was angry. But his anger was passion, she realised with a heart-thumping reality.

'Compromise. We'll do it together, sweet one,' he told her sensually, the words loaded with meaning.

'We'll do everything together—cooking, eating, making love——'

'Victor!'

It was a feeble struggle, the one she put up in protest, the one she tried to use to get out of his passionate embrace. But the sun and the heat and the long drowsy sleep under the palm had left her with little strength, and she was weakly floundering, as that poor fish had done earlier.

His kiss didn't flounder, though. His lips went straight to their desired target—her own warm lips—and they lingered so endearingly that she felt an alien weakness rippling through her. His arms held her tightly to him, and the coiled hair on his chest that she had admired just moments ago adhered to her heated flesh as if it was pre-destined. His legs, in shorts, were bare and strong, and the pleasure of his naked flesh on hers was immense.

She inwardly reeled with the contact of his mouth on hers, the forceful way he grasped her to him, the fury of desire it roused in her own body. It was a feeling like no other, a fear and yet an enormous excitement, a rush of passion and desire, and yet it made her feel strangely, softly sensuous. It was all a huge flood of conflicting raging emotions—rapids of confusion, white water of doubt and danger—and yet she could do nothing to stop it. The feeling of need coursed through and she let it, because he would never know if she held herself in check.

She drew back at last, her breath catching in her throat at the look of wanting in his eyes. Was she giving herself away so openly too? Could he see what she thought she could keep hidden inside and away from him?

He made no attempt to draw her back into his arms. They both got to their feet. 'I'm starving,' he said as if that passionate embrace had never happened. 'I'll light the fire and you find some leaves to wrap that fish in to cook it.'

He headed towards the house, leaving Christie standing, slightly trembling under the palm tree, a skirmish of sand at her feet where they had lain. His stride was steady, in control, not at all shaken by what had happened. And what exactly had happened? He had kissed her, again, but this time they were in a different environment, one she couldn't run away from. But he had known that when he'd brought her here—that there was no escape.

But she did want to escape, because what was on his mind was making her feel so peculiar. He wanted to make love to her and she probably wanted to make love to him too, and there was nothing to stop them, only her very female reasoning of not wanting to be used, not wanting to be taken for a fleeting few days of pleasure and then dropped because they had their own lives to lead once back in civilisation.

She was kneeling by the pile of sun-blanched driftwood when he came back, trying to heap it into a pile ready to be lit, but her hands were so unsteady that it kept toppling over.

'I don't even know you,' she murmured as he knelt down beside her to rearrange the pile. He struck a match and set fire to the bundle of dry twigs and leaves she had gathered to get the fire going, and sat back on his haunches to watch the flames crackle and blaze.

'And I don't know you, just enough to want you and take the risk that it will all work out,' he said quietly.

'There might not be anything to work out at the end of it all.'

'That's a risk we'll have to take. It's a risk in any relationship.'

'But this wouldn't be a relationship; it *isn't* a relationship,' she insisted. 'You say you want to make love to me and . . . and maybe——'

'You want to make love to me too, so we're halfway there.'

'To having an affair?' Christie smiled and stared hard at the flames that were now flushing her cheeks. 'And then what? I don't even know where you live, how old you are, how you like your steaks cooked.'

He winced. 'Don't mention steaks; I could murder one at the moment. I hope this works,' he pondered as he raked the hot ashes and settled more wood on the top to make a good bed of hot ash to lay the fish on. 'Did you find any big leaves?'

Christie leaned behind her to lift the fish, tightly wrapped in some dark green waxy leaves she had found growing at the edge of the beach. 'These could be poisonous too,' she mumbled, handing him the leaf-packaged fish.

'We die together, then,' he uttered resignedly and then grinned at the sudden look of fear in her glazed eyes. 'Have confidence in me, Christie. I wouldn't put you at risk—or myself, come to that.' He settled the fish on to the bed of hot ashes and with a stick heaped more up the sides of the package.

'Meaning what—those leaves or what we were just talking about?'

'These leaves aren't poisonous and the other thing is always a risking thing anyway.'

'Having an affair?' she quizzed.

'I prefer to think of it as falling in love, not an affair.'

'That's a silly thing to say. Falling in love takes time, time we haven't had and time we haven't got,' she retorted.

'Four days is long enough to fall in love, four minutes is enough for some people, and some people take four months or even four years. Which of the four would you like to go for?'

Christie laughed. 'You can't predict these things— how long it takes to fall in love.'

'You can make a guess, though, drawing on past experience.'

'Not easy,' Christie said on a sigh. 'What about you? Are you a four-minute man?'

He laughed. 'Certainly not, I rate my libido higher than that.'

She tossed a tiny pink shell at his head. 'I didn't mean that! I mean how long does it take for you to fall in love?'

'You don't hear very well, do you? I've told you I've never been in love before.'

'Before what?' she asked daringly, teasingly.

He held her eyes. For a fraction of a second uncertainty seemed to glaze the darkness of his eyes, then he laughed. 'That one is too deep for me. Keep an eye on that while I go up to the house for some wine to wash this down with.'

'And some plates and forks and napkins and con-
diments, and you might as well bring the tin-opener
and a can of beans in case this all goes horribly
wrong,' she told him as she prodded the fish
suspiciously.

'No faith, that's your problem,' he muttered as he
ambled back to the house.

Christie sat in the sand, clutching her knees and
watching the sea curl rapturously along the sand, tiny
waves curling backwards and forwards, ending up in
the same place each time, a bit like her own curling
thoughts. In spite of everything she felt a pleasant
ease, a sort of contentment inside her. She wasn't
afraid of Victor, that she knew for sure. He wouldn't
do anything she didn't want. If she didn't want to
make love with him he wouldn't force her, but there
were other ways of putting pressure on her other than
brute force. Just being here with him, doing silly
things like baking this silly fish in silly leaves on the
beach with him, was an aphrodisiac in itself. Oh,
beware paradise, she took up his warning in an in-
cantation of her own. I don't want to be hurt, she
added to the lament; please don't let me be hurt.

'That was thoughtful of you, cooling the wine and
stocking the fridge with drinks and making the house
look so lovely with flowers.' He thudded a wicker
basket down on the sand next to her and proceeded
to unpack it.

'Will she mind, this Delia?'

'Not at all. She's like that, a very giving person.'

'How giving?' Christie asked airily.

'Very giving.'

'It's that sort of relationship, is it?'

'What sort?'

'A giving sort.'

'A sexual giving sort?'

Did she really want to know? The ache inside her confirmed she did. 'Yes, a sexual giving sort of giving.'

He laughed. 'Why do women always want to know these things?'

'Why do men think it unimportant?'

He sat back and studied her, that penetrating look again. 'Because it is unimportant,' he said slowly. 'My past and your past has no bearing on our future.'

'It has too,' she protested, watching as he picked up the wine and proceeded to uncork it. 'That's if we have a future. I mean . . . I mean . . .'

'You mean you think we might have one—a future, that is?'

Christie was brave, very brave, and pushy went with brave. 'You said we had. You said, back in Grenada, "It rather clears the dross for our future relationship".'

'Yes, but this is the future for us now. The present is the future as looked at from the past.'

'You are a tricky devil, aren't you?' she said rhetorically as he poured two glasses of wine and handed her one. She felt a little stung that he obviously thought this was it, the future he had suggested, to go no further.

'You seem to think I am. I think I'm a very straight sort of guy. I don't think my past relationships have any bearing on what is happening between us now, nor yours either.'

'Well, you're a rare breed of man, then. I could be the hooker of the year and it wouldn't matter to you if you really believe what you say.'

'It wouldn't matter if I was aiming to have my evil way with you and then just dump you and sail off into the sunset, and besides, I know you're not the hooker of the year. If you were you'd have floored Paul by now.'

She mused on that for a few seconds, her heart pulsing slowly as she mused that maybe he did see them progressing beyond this short time together. He sounded as if he wanted them to go on beyond the sunset, but he would give that impression, wouldn't he? He'd hardly admit to wanting a four-day fling— full stop.

'Talking of Paul, does he know we're here? Did you leave word that we were going off for a few days?' A change of subject was a good idea at this point, and it was something that had been at the back of her mind ever since they had left. She didn't want Paul and Michelle worrying at their sudden disappearance.

He sipped his white wine before speaking. 'I left a note for Paul, telling him I'd fallen hopelessly in love with you and you with me and we just wanted to be alone together and we'd be back for the wedding.'

Christie didn't believe that for a minute, so she didn't allow herself a buzz of pleasure at the thought, but she did believe he wouldn't have left without telling someone where they were and when they were coming back.

'That's something, I suppose,' she murmured absently and sipped at her wine. 'I smell burning.'

Victor turned his attentions to the fish and gingerly turned it over with a fork and a spatula he'd brought down from the house. He was so engrossed in his task that Christie was able to study him without being noticed. She badly wanted to know so much about him, but he seemed so reticent, parrying her questions and suggestions with great skill and dexterity. But she was used to his sort, used to interviewing people and getting them to open up their inner feelings.

'Who was your father, then?' she asked bluntly. Sometimes it was the only way, straight to the heart of the matter with a pitchfork.

'My father?' he muttered, really concentrating hard on the fish, which seemed to be doing nicely by the mouth-watering smell it was giving off.

'You said you were a bastard and you don't carry the Tarrat name, so you must carry your father's. Lascelles sounds very aristocratic, so was your father nobility or something?'

He laughed. 'My mother—Paul's mother's sister—was an actress. Not very successful. I suspect my father was one of my mother's thespian friends. I don't even think my mother ever knew for sure. She lived in a world of her own, a world of unreality. She was a rebel, a free spirit. The Isadora Duncan of the fifties. She left England in the late fifties, convinced she was going to make a name for herself in Hollywood. She called herself Laura Lascelles, said it had a theatrical ring about it. It tolled no bells for her.' His eyes darkened, not in anger but sadness for the memory. 'Poor love was a born loser. She died seven years ago, in a backstage dressing-room in

Chicago, the way she would have wanted to go. A trouper to the end.'

'She sounds fascinating,' Christie murmured, 'and a good mother. You're a successful lawyer, so she obviously gave you a good start in life, in spite of everything.'

He sighed. 'Yes, she did,' he admitted. 'Though it was unorthodox. We toured a lot and when she could afford it she'd get me a tutor, the rest of the time we lived in an apartment in New York and I caught up on my schooling there. She called her touring my "education of life", and it was that for sure.' He grinned ruefully. 'Do I sound interesting enough for you to give me an interview?'

Christie smiled. 'A TV interview would be too mundane. I think your story would make a very successful Hollywood movie.'

'A bit dated, though. So what about you? Any skeletons in the cupboard?'

Christie shook her head. 'Not one. Very conventional upbringing. My parents are both in publishing and still live in middle-class mediocrity, splitting their time between Dorset and Bloomsbury. Nothing very sensational happens in their lives, unless you call endless publishing parties sensational. I went to university and then straight into broadcasting and just recently joined a new television franchise company. I get to travel more and the work is fascinating.'

'You'd have had to give all that up if you had married Paul.'

Christie looked at him quizzically. 'Would I?'

He nodded. 'I think so. Paul doesn't want competition in his life. It's why he and Michelle are so well suited. She'll be happy organising cocktail parties and domestic trivia for him for evermore. You wouldn't be happy doing that, would you?'

Christie had never thought about it. Her relationship with Paul had never got that far. It was obvious that Victor knew more about his cousin than she did. A while back that would have mattered; now it didn't.

'On reflection, no, because Paul wasn't the one, but who knows how I will feel when I do fall in love and my lover demands domestic trivia, *if* he demands it?'

For a moment, as Victor topped up their wine glasses, she allowed herself a small fantasy, putting herself in the position of being in love with Victor, being his lover. Would she give up her career for him? The fantasy came surprisingly easily, but the question was impossible to answer.

'W-would you demand it?' she asked at last.

He didn't even look at her, just stared stoically at the leaves spiralling smoke up from the hot ashes. 'I don't know. It's something I've never considered.'

'So you've never had a close enough relationship to wonder, maybe?'

He smiled and turned his head to look at her. 'Still trying to find out my previous love-life?'

Christie shrugged and set about laying out the plates and napkins on the sand. Paul had given her his interpretation of what he thought Victor's love-life was like—that he wasn't exactly the parish priest, but he didn't let women get to him—but she'd rather find out for herself. 'You intrigue me and I have an insatiable curiosity about people, probably why I do what I do so well.'

'In other words you're plain old nosy.'

She laughed. 'Something like that.'

'I think Moby Dick here must be done by now,' he said as he probed it with the sharp tip of a knife.

Christie's probing hadn't been as effective as that knife. Still she didn't know if he'd had anyone serious in his life. Usually when people were reticent about something it concealed a wound, yet he had not held anything back about his wayward mother, which showed he had no hang-ups there. But maybe there were hang-ups and they were so deep-seated that they could never be budged. Perhaps he didn't even know about them himself, not consciously. Christie wondered if he knew how chauvinistic he sounded sometimes. Some men were unaware of it, some played on it for sport, some genuinely felt it, programmed from an early age by a narrow upbringing. There were many other reasons for men's attitudes to women, and she wondered where Victor's reasons lay, or maybe it was just her and the reaction she aroused in him. She had riled him from the very onset of their meeting and yet he still wanted her. Christie wished she'd paid more attention to psychology at university.

'Hey, this looks good,' he enthused after removing the package form the ashes, gingerly unwrapping it, and gently scraping the scales from the flesh. He held up a forkful of white meat for her to sample. 'Want to be the guinea-pig?'

'Why not?' she laughed, leaning forward on her knees and taking the mouthful. 'Hmm, ambrosia,' she muffled with her mouth full. She took the fork from him and plunged in for another forkful. 'Try it.'

Their eyes locked as he opened his mouth to be fed, and Christie felt a deep flush creep up her neck. His hand came up and clasped around the hand that held the fork. He seemed to hold it for a lifetime, and held her eyes for another lifetime.

He swallowed at last, made no comment about the succulent fish, but simply said very softly, 'Now I understand the temptation Paul was exposed to. There is something very sensual about being fed.'

'He was feeding me, don't forget, and I didn't find it very sensual.'

'It frightened you into scampering off like a petrified rabbit. But you didn't flee when I did it just now.' His voice was low and loaded.

Christie felt colour rise to her cheeks again, but she smiled, trying to deflect away from that. 'It's all to do with the cradle, the primeval need to be fed and nurtured by somebody else. Enjoying it in adulthood probably shows a very immature, demanding nature and . . . a bed-wetter to boot.'

Victor was still laughing as he picked up another fork and tossed her a napkin. Together they demolished the fish in much less time than it had taken to cook it. They drank the rest of the wine, too, the whole litre bottle. Christie felt decidedly woozy as she drained the last drop.

'And no washing-up,' she sighed dreamily, flopping back into the sand and cupping her hands behind her head. She watched the bright blue sky through the fronds of the palm above her head and knew she was in paradise, a true paradise, a paradise of contentment of mind and spirit. She closed her eyes. I like you very much, she mused to herself, you, Victor Lascelles. I like you for the food you hunted for me, cooked for me, fed to me. I like you because you make me laugh, because you're different, because you're you. I could fall in love with you, I might already be in love with you and . . . and I think I've drunk too much wine in the heat of the day.

'Don't, Victor,' she murmured languidly, feeling him brush something against her thigh. 'Don't spoil it. It's too soon . . . I need time . . . Victor!'

She shot to a sitting position, but Victor was nowhere in sight. Her eyes opened in horror at the sight of a small army of nut-brown crabs feasting on the remains of the fish bone and tail, which lay in its bed of burnt leaves in the sand. And dear God . . . the mother of all crabs was hanging on to the frill of the bottom half of her yellow bikini by the biggest pincer she had seen in her life!

'Victor!' she screamed hysterically, leaping to her feet and doing a fine rendition of the Mexican hat dance and waving her hands frantically in the air as if they were on fire, all to no avail as the monster just hung on. 'Victor, for God's sake get it off!'

He came pelting down to the beach, face drawn, then his features softened with mirth. He skidded to a halt in front of her.

'You get it off—slip it off.'

'Slip what off?' she screamed, hopping about, desperately trying to keep the thing from touching the bare flesh of her thigh as it swung perilously close.

'The bikini bottom. Just step out of it——'

'Don't be so bloody ridiculous! If I do I'll be half naked!'

'Better than being eaten alive.' He was laughing, highly amused at her predicament.

'This isn't funny,' she raged, hot tears of panic stinging her eyes. 'Get it off, I beg you, because I'm going to... going to faint if you don't!'

He stepped towards her, still grinning. Christie was still hopping around and the crab was still hanging on for grim death.

'Hold still,' he warned. With one hand he held her bottom, holding her steady as she tried so very hard to keep still. A new panic raged now, at his touch on her flesh, the warmth and the firmness of that touch. Was she mad? She was dicing with death here at the hands of a cannibal crab and now she was panicking at Victor's touch. Get your priorities right!

She felt dizzy and sick as Victor tried, unsuccessfully, to part the determined crab from the fabric frill. 'She's got a fine pair of pincers there,' he commented with interest, as if he were on a biological study in some ancient archipelago and had discovered a new species of crustacean unknown to man.

'Just stop fooling around and get it off, bloody Darwin!' she screamed hysterically. 'You shouldn't have left all that fish debris around...and where were you when I needed you? Damn you ... this is all your fault!'

'I was working,' he told her through gritted teeth, his amusement gone now, and she didn't know if it was because of the reluctant crab or annoyance that she was blaming him for it. 'This whole wretched

Caribbean extravaganza is costing me dearly,' he added irritably.

Christie went cold inside, astonished at the disappointment that iced through her at that bald statement. She almost forgot the plight she was in.

'There, easy does it. She's a tough little so-and-so.' He was holding the crab by its middle, gently trying to tear it away without hurting it. Christie did not— *would* not—acknowledge that he was doing it with the crab's best interest at heart.

'It would be a *she*, wouldn't it?' she bit out crazily. 'It couldn't be a *he*; only a *she* could be so truculent and obstinate!'

His eyes suddenly blazed up to hers; he was quite surprised at her outburst, but not willing to question why and not willing to rein in the anger of his own. 'Don't be so damned childish, Christie. You're acting crazy. It won't hurt you.'

Suddenly she was free and Victor released her and set the crab down on the sand, where it scurried for cover.

'What the hell are you crying for?' His voice was outraged at the sight of the tears spilling down her cheeks.

Christie was outraged that she had allowed them to fall. 'Because...because... Oh, to hell with you...you pig!'

She spun around in the sand and ran full pelt for the house, telling herself she'd had too much to drink, had stayed in the sun too long, that fish didn't agree with her, and she wasn't particularly enraptured with man-eating crabs swinging from her bikini bottom, and that it was nothing—absolutely nothing—to do with Victor's 'wretched Caribbean extravaganza', which was irritatingly holding up his career and very obviously costing him mega amounts of dollars!

CHAPTER SEVEN

CHRISTIE lay on her bed with the fattest headache she had endured for years. She reached for the bottle of water Victor had put by her bedside, shakily poured herself a glassful, and swallowed it in a long, cool draught.

She slumped back against the pillows and realised it was dark already, dark except for a candle burning in a glass bowl next to the water.

She vaguely remembered Victor coming into her room to ask if she was OK and then going away for the water. She didn't remember him coming back.

That was a lesson well learnt: wine and sun didn't mix.

'Feel better now?'

She looked up, remembering she had torn off her bikini after she had stormed up from the beach and had slid into her satin robe before throwing herself down on her bed in misery. It was still intact, covering all it needed to cover. She eased up and leaned back against the pillows again and her eyes focused on him as he pulled up a chair and sat by the bed as if he were visiting a patient in hospital. Her heart plummeted at that. If—*if* he had warm intentions towards her he would have plumped himself down on the edge of the bed, but what she had learned about him so far was that he was quite a reserved person—sometimes.

'I've got a fearful headache, and, before you start lecturing. I've learnt my lesson. Too much sun and wine and——'

'And there's a fearful storm brewing, and that could be a contributing factor to your fearful headache,' he said kindly and with humour.

'And don't be so beastly patronising. I've got a stinking hangover and that's it!'

Just then there was a snap of lightning that brightened the room, a thud of thunder in the distance and an instant pounding of rain on the wooden roof above their heads. Miraculously the pressure in her temples seemed to ease.

'How long do you think the storm will last?' she asked.

'How long is a piece of string?'

Christie gave him a wan smile. 'I suppose that was a silly question.'

'The rain brings the silly season, so here's another silly question: what in heaven's name were you so het up about on the beach earlier?'

Christie shifted her position and then stilled herself, because that shift might have looked like a squirm of embarrassment to his perceptive eye, which it was actually. She was cross with herself for feeling so put down when he had said he'd been working. It was quite ridiculous that she should feel that he wasn't giving her his undivided attention after all he had led her to believe—that he wanted to get to know her better, that he wanted to enjoy her. It was a disappointment she was trying to come to terms with.

'I thought that was pretty obvious,' she breathed. 'I was about to be eaten alive by a fearsome crustacean and you were treating it as a huge joke.'

'I rescued you, didn't I?' There was a slight smile at the edge of his mouth, but not a full-blown grin. It was as if he wasn't sure how deeply the encounter had affected her and he didn't want to push his luck.

'Eventually,' she agreed. 'But not half quickly enough. By the time you did I was in trauma. I woke up to find myself surrounded by creepy-crawlies with talons or pincers or whatever they call them.'

'I'm sorry, but I'm afraid you'll have to get used to them. There's an abundance on the island. It's so infrequently inhabited that wildlife is virtually undisturbed, which is a nice thought, isn't it?'

He was making her feel guilty now, as if she were one of those women who had the vapours at the sight of anything with more than two legs.

'I've nothing against the wildlife,' she told him tightly. 'I just don't want it swinging from my bikini bottom, thank you.'

'There was a crab with good taste.' He said it with a broad smile to cheer her up, but it fell far short of Christie's barrier of happiness.

Christie swung her legs off the bed and got up. A gecko scuttled up the wall next to the bed, its fat little hands sprawled out like a child's to grip the panelling. It made Christie jump and she drew her arms about her.

'It won't hurt you——'

'I know it won't!' Christie snapped at him fiercely. 'It just startled me, that's all. I know all about them. They eat the midges and the cockroaches, and they say that a tropical home without a gecko isn't a happy home.'

'Well, that little sod is out of place, then, isn't he?' he snapped back, suddenly on his feet too and glaring at her as if *she* were something undesirable with more than two legs.

Christie swept her tousled hair from her face and glared back at him. 'I've had enough of this!' she exploded. 'We should never have come. It was a ridiculous idea! The weather is nonsense, the wildlife nonsense. I'm sick of it already. Take me back to Grenada—now! If you don't, I'll take the boat and *pilot* myself back. I couldn't do a worse job of it than you did . . . What are you doing?'

He had grabbed her arm and was *piloting* her across the room to the veranda before she could stop him.

'What the hell do you think that is?' he grated, waving his other hand at the rain that was coming down like a continuous sheet of iron filings. 'This isn't some April shower over the South Downs, you know. It's a raging tropical storm with seas like boiling cauldrons. Want to take your chance, do you? Well, off you go—*bon voyage*—but first you'll have to drag the boat back down to the water, and good luck, because it took me two hours to get it up the beach while you were sleeping your hangover off!'

He released her and strode off along the veranda to the sitting-room, his shoulders so tense that they looked about to snap with rage.

Christie watched him, her insides boiling like the sea must be in this raging storm. But her rage was tempered by the thought of his hauling the boat to safety. Even with the winch she'd seen by the jetty it must have been a difficult single-handed task.

She went back into her bedroom, dressed in a cool cerise pareu, and brushed out her hair before going into the sitting-room. He was seated at the coffee-table, working his way through a sheaf of papers, and didn't even look up when she swished past to the kitchen.

'I'll make supper,' she told him meekly, only she found it already prepared in the fridge—a bowl of fresh salad and a selection of canned cold meats cut into slices. He'd arranged it on the plates to look appetising, and it did, and he'd waited for her to arouse herself before eating himself, and she was mortally sorry for snapping at him so irritably.

'Thank you for making the supper,' she said in a quiet voice. 'And I'm sorry for being such a bitch.'

He looked up at her with eyes strained from reading through his work in only a dim light from a hurricane lamp set on the table.

'Sexual tension,' he said, holding her eyes till she could stand it no longer and averted hers skywards.

'It would be, wouldn't it? It couldn't be anything as simple as too much sun, wine and sheer exhaustion after being dragged out of my bed this morning at the crack of dawn for this ridiculous escapade.'

'I'm sure they are all contributing factors, but not the key one. You need what I need, and a bit of good old-fashioned honesty wouldn't go amiss. Do you still want to leave?' he asked.

'I do, but I won't. I wouldn't miss this for the world, proving you wrong!' Trouble was, could she prove wrong something that was undoubtably right, and did she want to? 'Are you ready to eat now or would you rather wait till you've finished your work?'

He shuffled the papers together. 'Now's as good a time as any. I've set the table outside on the veranda.'

'Won't we get wet?'

'It's covered and we won't unless the wind changes.'

Funny how they had this ability to carry on normally when everything was far from the norm. Christie carried the food outside. He'd laid the rattan table with a linen cloth, and the silver sparkled in the glow from a single white candle in a bowl on the table, like the one he had thoughtfully put by her bed. He lit other candles behind glass shields that hung from the side of the house. The flowers she had picked earlier were vibrant in the glow from the lights.

It all looked incredibly beautiful, a secret, enchanting place, enigmatic because of the location and the rain that was perpetually thrumming on the roof. It was so hot and humid, and that added to the unreality of it all.

'I feel as if I'm dreaming,' Christie said as she sat down and he sat across from her.

'Or hallucinating,' he suggested with a small smile as he poured her a glass of water.

'Is that why we're not having wine tonight?' She smiled as she said it to show she was relaxed now. Though she wasn't exactly relaxed, just a little less tense, which was quite different.

'Yes, I think you've had enough for one day. I couldn't stand you turning on me like a Valkyrie again tonight.'

'Was I that bad?'

'Impossible, but if you make it up to me this evening I'll allow you a rum punch later.'

He started to dish up the food and Christie leaned forward and took the servers from his hands.

'That's my job,' she said and carried on where she had interrupted him. 'And how am I supposed to make it up to you tonight, or is that a question that doesn't warrant an answer?'

'Well, it was a question that suggests quite a heavy commitment that I don't think either of us is ready for yet.'

Christie raised a brow. 'Are we talking about the same thing here?'

'I guess so. I want to get to know you better before we do anything rash like falling into bed together.'

'I think I should have said that first. It's the sort of thing women say. It makes a change for it to come from the man.'

'I think you've been unfortunate in your choice of men.'

'There haven't been that many,' she admitted ruefully. 'A fling or two at uni...and men in the media do nothing for my pulse-rate. Most are having affairs with their own egos or looking for a mirror image of themselves.'

He laughed softly. 'Is that why you fell so heavily for Paul, because he was different?'

'Fell so heavily,' she repeated in a musing fashion, spearing another slice of meat from the plate and shifting it to his. 'That sounds as if I fell off the top of a cliff.'

'And landed with a painful bump when it didn't work out.'

She shook her head as she swallowed. 'It wasn't really like that. I was greatly attracted to him, yes, because he was different. Paul isn't in the least bit affected. I know he goes over the top sometimes, but he's quite a natural really, though I expect you know that.'

He nodded. 'I do. He's the one who has brought me into the family from the cold. Go on. What were you saying?'

Christie wanted to pursue that, but she shelved it for the moment, because she wanted to say what she needed to say.

'I landed painfully, not because of him jilting me... well, yes, part of it was that, but a lot of the angst was because it made me question the frailty of my own emotions.' She smiled and toyed with a tomato on her plate. 'I made a mistake. It could have been disastrous. Supposing Paul had asked me to marry him? I would have done months back and it would have been a ghastly mistake. My emotions could have led me to make the biggest mistake of my life. It all boils down to not really knowing yourself.' She shrugged. 'Here I am, successful in my working life, a walking disaster in my private life. I don't know myself and that's where most of the angst lies; odd, isn't it?'

'Why should it be odd? People live their lives not ever getting to know themselves.'

'But where love is concerned, one should know oneself.'

He grinned and leaned towards her conspiratorially. 'Now if that was the case I wouldn't be where I am today.'

Christie laughed. 'So you won't support the cause for getting to know oneself better?'

'For myself I wholeheartedly agree with you, but for the rest of the world out there ignorance is bliss, or I'd be out of business.'

'It's a shame, isn't it, that people make such mistakes in their lives, marry the wrong people, think they are in love and then find they're not? You must see a lot of heartbreak.'

He nodded. 'I do. The worst thing is when two people are still in love and shouldn't even be contemplating divorce, but they seem to be on a roller-coaster, not able to communicate with each other because of suppressed feelings, and egged on by so-called friends, usually ones who are divorced themselves and swear it's the best thing they've ever done when secretly they are dying of loneliness. Then when children are involved——'

Impulsively Christie reached out and closed her hand over his. 'Don't,' she said huskily. 'This is far too serious a subject to be talking about on such a beautiful night.'

Just then a bolt of lightning flashed the skies above and they both burst out laughing.

Later, much later, Victor mixed two long glasses of rum punch, and as they sat on the veranda and watched the storm rage fitfully over the Caribbean sea Christie knew that before Victor Lascelles had appeared on her screen of life it had all been rather vacant.

Somehow this storm and him sitting across from her had intensified it, made her look back and wonder what it was all about, this living thing. She wanted him, she realised, not a passing wanting but a progressive wanting. She wanted to know him now and tomorrow and the day after. Was it love? How would she ever know after what they had just been talking about? But she felt an intensity inside her that suggested that she hadn't exercised as much caution as she had hoped she might if the occasion ever rose again. How sublime to say that this feeling was different so she wouldn't. But perhaps he was right about the sexual tension; her insides were balling with it now, and that was a bit of old-fashioned honesty to be going on with.

'I was furious with you this afternoon on the beach,' she said at last.

'I know,' he murmured. 'I was there.'

'It's because you weren't there before that I was so mad. You said this wretched Caribbean extravaganza was costing you.'

'And you were needled because you expected my undivided attention all the while we are here.'

Her eyes widened. He seemed to know her better than she knew herself.

'Yes,' she admitted in a small voice. 'Just as I was beginning to enjoy myself you copped out.'

'I copped out because you did. You fell asleep so I left you to rest while I got on with some work. I don't think that is unreasonable, do you?'

'No, of course not,' she said resignedly. 'I'd have done the same thing; it's just that——'

'You were disappointed?'

She eyed him bravely. 'Yes, I was, but you made me feel as if I was a nuisance, that this whole charade down here is a nuisance. That you would much rather be back in the States working.'

'I would,' he said quietly, and Christie's disappointment deepened till it was a physical pain deep inside her. The disappointment was obviously mirrored in her eyes, and he smiled and reached out for her hand across the table. His touch was warm and light, conciliatory and little else, and it did nothing to put Christie's heart at ease. 'But if I hadn't come to my cousin's wedding I would never have met you, so there are enormous compensations.'

'Am I supposed to be flattered by that?' she murmured, lowering her lashes.

'Flattered, yes; swayed, no. I want you in my bed with your head screwed on the right way, not turned by a few flattering words.'

'Is that important, then?'

His eyes narrowed. 'I shall pretend I didn't hear that.'

Christie refused to be cowed into submission by that. She withdrew her hand from under his. 'And I shall pretend I didn't hear that, because you're evading the issue. I'm beginning to wonder what you are expecting from all this enforced isolation. You say you want me, but you're implying you want me under your own obscure terms. I suppose my feelings don't come under scrutiny.'

'Your feelings are what all this is about,' he said darkly.

'Oh, and how do you make that out?'

'Quite easily. You're the one with the instability; you're the one who is in love with someone one minute and the next dismissing it as if it was a temporary aberration of the mind.'

Christie sat silent for a few minutes, twirling her glass in her fingers, but not touching a drop of the spicy rum punch. She should be hurt by that, but it was the truth. But what had her heart thudding dangerously was that he seemed to want a deeper relationship than she had anticipated, or it could be just his way of ensuring that whatever they did together would be with the intensity he desired. This wasn't a normal run-of-the-mill man who wanted a night of 'wham, bam, thank you ma'am'; he was thinking of something more intense. He wanted it all, absolute submission, no holds barred, the Kama Sutra in Technicolor—and then what? The ultimate put-down from a man she saw as a misogynist—fall in love with me and then I'll show you what pain is.

God, she could see it all now. He was on a one-way woman-destroying mission powered by his unorthodox upbringing. A woman-hater because of the failings of his mother?

And yet as she raised her eyes to his to see him watching her thoughtfully she wondered if she was being cruel in judging him that way. It could be the very reverse. He could be longing for true love, something his mother had never had. He could be wanting to be so sure about a relationship that he wasn't prepared to take unnecessary risks to get it.

'I made a mistake,' she murmured and shrugged. 'It could have been worse. I could be sitting here now asking you what to do with an ailing marriage.'

'If you were married I can assure you you wouldn't be here,' he said on a smile. 'I wouldn't have brought you.'

'So why did you, apart from keeping me out of the wedding couple's way?'

'I've already told you that. You know it, but you seem incapable of understanding it, so until you do I can't add anything more.' He looked at her, met her eyes, and held them.

Christie raised her glass to her lips, but didn't take her eyes from his. She swallowed and slowly lowered the glass to the table. 'You said you wanted to enjoy me, you say you want to bed me, but you leave a hell of a lot unsaid, which worries me.'

'Like what?'

'Why, for one thing.'

'I think that's obvious. I find you incredibly sexy, I fancy you like crazy, I want to touch every part of your delectable body, I want to be inside you, and I want to wake up in the morning with you in my arms and do it all over again.'

Heat raged inside her, but she willed herself to stay cool.

'Is that all?'

He looked taken aback for a second and then he smiled. 'I think that's enough to be going on with. Now why don't you make some admissions of your own? And we might start to get somewhere.'

'Do you want the absolute truth?' she asked, and knew he would say yes, and she was prepared to give it to him, because words were easy.

'I want you too. I want everything you want. I want to go to bed with you, but I might want to go to bed with you again and again. I also happen to like you, which I think is one up on your feelings for me, but I've found out that I'm not very good at relationships, so my needs are tempered with caution. You see, this is more than just a question of satisfying primeval urges; this could have consequences and those consequences have to be considered——'

'Like falling in love?'

Christie laughed cynically. 'What the hell would you know about falling in love?'

'And you're the expert, are you?' he said with irony.

'*Touché*. So neither of us has been in love——'

'But we could be now,' he suggested.

His words hung in the air alongside the suffocating humidity, just hung there waiting, waiting, waiting.

Christie stared at him, despising him for that. He'd made that ridiculous suggestion to make it easier for him to bed her, thinking that she would be swayed by words of love. She wanted to be angry, but the rage stayed trapped in her throat. Slowly she formed words and they slid from her lips icily. 'Love in such a short space of time? How come you've got this knack of opening your mouth and spouting such trash? I thought you were quite bright——'

'And I thought you were too,' he interrupted darkly.

'I don't understand you, I really don't.'

'I know you don't,' he said quietly. 'That's what makes it so interesting.' He stood up and pushed his chair back. 'Coffee?'

'N-no, thank you.' She stood up too, determinedly. The rain had eased and she stared out into the black night, wanting to be out there in that blackness, alone. 'I'm going for a walk——'

'It's still raining. You'll get drenched.'

'So I'll get drenched.'

'I'm not coming after you, if that's what you're hoping.'

'Go to hell!' she fired back and ran, far away from him, because he made her so mad!

She ran down the leafy path that led to the beach. It was so pitch-dark that she couldn't see, but the path was straight, and once she was on the wet sands the clouds parted and the moon shone brightly for her. She stood on the shoreline, letting the swirling water cover her feet and lap around the hem of her pareu. It was cooler here and she stood motionless in the moonlight and let the rain wash over her till her hair hung limp and wet across her shoulders.

She didn't understand that man and she so badly wanted to. She despised him so much for talking so idly of love when it couldn't be anything but desire. She covered her face with her hands. But for her she knew it was more than desire, because if it were simply that she would be in bed with him now, not thinking of those damned consequences she had sounded off about, as if she knew all that she was talking about.

God, he was so right—what did she know? She knew nothing about love or even men, especially not this one.

He slid his arms around her waist and turned her into him, and his mouth covered hers heatedly. Christie struggled for a second till he released her mouth but tightened his grip on her.

'I thought you said you wouldn't come after me,' she panted, trying to struggle out of his arms.

'I changed my mind.'

'Well, I haven't changed mine!' she blurted fiercely. 'I came down here because I want to be alone, so allow me that freedom at the very least.'

'People wander a moonlit beach because they're troubled——'

'Don't be so damned ridiculous! What were you troubled about back in Grenada, then, when you were wandering the beach like a lost soul that first night— where the next juicy divorce case was coming from?' She struggled so hard that she was free, and stepped back, deeper into the water.

His hand snaked out and grasped her back, hard against his soaking wet body. She couldn't see the anger in his face, but she felt it in the tension of his body.

'I was troubled all right,' he rasped angrily. 'I'd met this woman, you see. For once in my life I'd met a woman whom I wanted so badly I was sick to the gut with need. But that woman was unobtainable, out of reach——'

'So now I see it all,' Christie cried back at him, so deeply hurt that he had wanted that woman in his past so badly, so crazed with jealousy that she wanted to hurt and hurt him back. 'And you wanted to punish for that, didn't you? Any woman who came your way. You couldn't have her, so you have a vendetta against all women. Oh, it accounts for your treatment of me, your damned chauvinistic attitude, all that garbage about wanting to enjoy... All you want to do is *destroy*!'

His grip on her arms tightened till her arms went numb, and he shook her. 'And then I found out she *was* available and I still couldn't have her because she was still knotted up about another man——'

'Oh, and that made it worse, didn't it? Your charm didn't work . . . your charisma just didn't turn her on, and that must have made your ego boil . . . Well, what the hell has all that do with me? Why punish *me*?'

The moonlight lit his eyes then and she saw such raw savagery there that her insides went weak with fear.

'That wretched woman was you, Christie!' he raged. 'And you're still not free, still not available, and that's why *you* knot me up!'

He let her go then, and thrust her away from him so harshly that she nearly stumbled back into the sea. He turned and strode back to the house. Christie stood with the sea swirling around her ankles, stunned into immobility. He'd been talking about *her*!

At last she found her voice, a small, creaky voice that somehow carried up the beach to halt him in his tracks.

'Victor!' she cried, stumbling after him. 'Victor, I . . .' She came to a stop in front of him, rain streaming from her face, her sopping wet pareu clinging provocatively to the curves of her naked body beneath it. 'I . . . I am free . . . I am available . . . Victor . . . I want you . . . I . . . I want whatever you want.'

He stood immobile in front of her, his body tense and ungiving, soaked through to the skin like her, his dark hair jet against his head, his eyes black and totally unreadable because of the thundery darkness again. No moon now to give her any indication of how he truly felt at her submission. Suddenly there was a terrible rumble of thunder given out as a reminder that the storm was far from abated. Then as the rain intensified brutally Victor swept her up into his arms and carried her back to the house.

He set her down in his bedroom, where only a solitary candle burned to give them light. But it was enough for Christie to see the burning desire in his eyes. He held her face, looking down into her eyes for a while, and neither of them spoke. He smoothed her wet hair from her cheeks and then lowered his heated mouth to hers.

Christie clung to him, all the fires of her passion already aglow, her need pulsing her wet skin till she trembled with the depth of her desire. She didn't want to think of those damning consequences; she didn't want to think of anything but Victor in her arms, loving her and wanting her.

The storm raged outside and a storm raged inside as they clung feverishly together, mouthing kisses across each other's faces, their lips drawing hungrily at the beads of water on their faces and hair. It was impossible to remove their wet clothes with anything other than a clawing desperation, but at last they were free, bodies trembling against each other as their naked flesh fused and their mouths sought each other's again.

Victor lifted her one more time, held her in his arms to look down into her face, before smiling and lowering her to the cool cotton of his bed. He towered over her, teasing her now by not lying with her immediately but just leaning over her to run his mouth and tongue the length of her body—her throat, her breasts, lingering for a while on her peaked nipples, drawing on them till she was moaning her need, then

the flat of her stomach, then the soft mound that
throbbed so achingly for so much more.

At last she could bear the teasing no longer and
reached for him, but didn't pull him down to the bed.
He held her head as she tasted him, let out small
moans of deep pleasure as she ran her tongue around
his marvellous arousal. Her pleasure was immense; a
joy that filled her heart to be so intimately loving him,
adoring the magnificence of his body as it shuddered
against her mouth.

He murmured something unintelligible, more a plea
of restraint than one of pleasure, and then he eased
away from her and lowered himself beside her,
clasping her against him and rolling her under him.
He slid his hand between her legs, and stroked her so
sensuously that she writhed under the touch, burning,
burning to be released. Their mouths touched, parted,
drew deeply on each other's silky inner sweetness,
grazed across their faces, hungrily, savagely, as their
need sped them deeper and deeper into a world of
hedonistic pleasure and pain.

They both gasped deeply when at last he could hold
back no longer and entered her with a deep, long
thrust that had the bed groaning under them. His drive
and strength thrust them higher and higher till the
sounds of passion filled the room, moans and gasps
of sheer delight that came unhindered from their
throats to vie with the roar of the storm that pounded
around the tiny island.

The sexual storm broke as Christie let go, trembling and shuddering against him, having the effect
of accelerating his own climax till they were writhing
in the throes of sweet, moist ecstasy, thrusting hard

against each other, desperate to cling on till the very last draining expulsion of liquid fire made them cry out with the force of the power that enveloped them.

And then the calm and the exquisite pleasure of soft caresses and small reassuring touches as they lay in each other's arms, sated, relaxed and dazed by the power of the feeling between them. No words needed to be spoken; nothing needed to be said. They simply let the heavy languidness fall around them till their hearts levelled and there was peace and silence.

CHAPTER EIGHT

'Do you like that?'

Christie roused herself from the deepest of sweet slumbers. It was light and quiet, no wind or rain to mar the peace, but then the light was gone as Victor's head blacked it out. He lowered his mouth to hers, but kept up the tantalising pressure of his fingers stroking her between her thighs. Oh, God, she was coming and it was too exquisite for words.

'That wasn't fair,' she murmured at last. 'I woke up too late.'

'You woke up just in time,' he grated in her ear as he hugged her tightly to him.

'I missed the preliminaries.'

'There weren't any; I'd only just started, you wanton hussy.'

She snuggled her mouth into his neck and murmured sleepily, 'Remind me I owe you one.'

With his thumb he lifted one of her eyelids and peered into her eye and then, satisfied that she was wide awake, he kissed the tip of her nose. 'I don't take IOUs; it's cash on delivery, or else.' He pressed himself against her and in delighted surprise she was suddenly wide awake.

His morning lovemaking was very different from his nocturnal performance. They had all the rest of the day for exquisite, intimate explorations and there was no rush, no rush till those impassioned explorations gave way to what they couldn't hold on to an agonising moment later.

Victor Lascelles was a perfect lover and Christie told him so as they lay in each other's arms, drifting again, languorously watching a humming-bird hovering in the heart of an hibiscus flower outside the open window. The sun was bright outside and the rain had coaxed delicious warm scents from the earth and the flowers, and they perfumed the room.

'And you're a very receptive lover,' he murmured softly in her ear. 'Like that hibiscus, giving your nectar so willingly.'

'I was a push-over, was I?' She laughed as she said it, because she didn't want him to think she was serious.

'No, I was. I had every intention of holding back from you longer.'

'There's a name for women who do that, but none for a man.'

'You'd better invent one, then,' he suggested teasingly.

She did, leaned towards him, and whispered it in his ear.

He laughed and rolled her over to slap her bottom. 'That was disgusting!'

One thing led to another and it was lunchtime before they surfaced, both ravenous.

'What's the shower arrangement here? I was scared to use it yesterday in case the water was rationed—is it?' Christie asked as she slid from the bed and with disgust picked up her still damp pareu from the floor and held it up 'twixt finger and thumb.

'You weren't wearing anything under that last night,' he observed from the bed, propped on one elbow as he watched her shaking it out.

'Would you believe I forgot to pack any underwear?'

He grinned. 'I'm beginning to wonder about you. You're right, you know. You hold down a successful career, but your private life is a little haywire, to say the least.'

'It might have something to do with you,' she grinned, coming back to the bed and kneeling on the edge to look down at him. She grew serious. 'Victor, what are we doing here?'

He looked puzzled, then grinned. 'Recovering after making the most incredible love.'

'Exactly. Do you know we've only known each other a couple of days, if that, and already we've——'

'Had a few rows, made a helluva lot of love, got drunk a bit . . . well, you have.' He grew serious then. 'Does that bother you, then, the lovemaking bit so soon?'

Christie lowered her lashes. It bothered her like crazy, but to admit it would sound so very female and so very old-fashioned.

'The time span between meeting someone and falling into bed with them is totally irrelevant if it's right, Christie, and it is right, you know, because neither of us would have let it happen if it wasn't.'

She smiled and raised her lashes to look at him. 'You make me feel very gauche, do you know that? I thought I had my life together, but you make me feel I haven't even touched the tip of it yet. Since I met you I've acted like some...some stupid naïve teenager. I mean I should have seen what was going on with Paul and Michelle, but I didn't. I should have known how you felt about me, but I...' Her voice gave out. But she didn't know how he felt about her, not truly.

Victor smoothed his hand along her thigh. 'I'm crazy about you,' he told her tenderly, as if he knew what had stopped her—uncertainty. He bent to kiss her knee and her hand went to the top of his head to smooth over his tousled hair.

'And I think I'm crazy about you,' she whispered and bit her lip, because his head was bent and he couldn't see her face and she needed that sharp little pain to remind herself to be careful. She could end up with a broken heart here, an agony that she had never felt before, though she had kidded herself she had with Paul. That was how much this Victor Lascelles had unsettled her; everything in her life that had gone before was a void of nothingness.

'Forget the shower,' he murmured as he lifted his head and pulled her down beside him. 'I don't want you to wash away your love scent.'

'I thought you were hungry,' she laughed softly as she wrapped her arms around his neck.

'I am,' was all he said as his mouth closed over hers.

'I've got one!' Christie screamed in excitement. 'What do I do, what do I do?'

The boat was tipping recklessly as she leapt around with excitement, trying to control the rod as it bowed and bucked with the weight of the fish she'd hooked.

'Easy, now,' Victor said soothingly, coming to stand behind her. He wrapped his arms around her to grasp the rod. 'Reel it in gently, gently.'

She was so excited that she couldn't. Her fingers tightened around the rod and she let him reel it for her. She felt the pressure of his body hard against her back and marvelled that she could be so doubly aroused. Catching the fish was a thrill, the contact of his body another, and it was difficult to say which rocked her the most.

'Oh, it's huge,' she giggled in excitement.

'I've never had any complaints before——'

'The fish, you idiot!' she screamed with laughter.

It was twice the size of the one he had caught that first day, and as Victor landed it on the deck of the boat Christie covered her face and cried out, 'Throw it back! I can't bear it. It's a creature and doesn't deserve to be eaten!'

He was still laughing when minutes later she uncovered her face to look down at the lifeless fish at her feet.

'You wouldn't think anything of it if it came packaged from the supermarket.'

'I know,' she breathed and slumped down on to the deck in a fit of exhaustion. 'Hypocritical, aren't I? But I've never caught a meal before. It's a bit strange, an odd feeling. I feel goosey all over.' She shivered and hugged herself.

Victor shifted the fish aside with his foot and joined her down on the deck, folding her into his arms and holding her. 'Let me ungoose you, then.' His lips covered hers, and her protest was very small and ineffectual and lay deep in her throat, where it stayed unsaid.

Later they lay sprawled on the deck of the boat bobbing on the sea, the yellow umbrella giving them welcome shade from the hot sun. Victor had one arm around her naked shoulders; the other supported his head as he dozed. She turned her head slightly so she could look at him as he rested. These days with him had somersaulted her mind till it spun with love for him. She was more than crazy about him now; she was so deeply in love that it hurt.

They hadn't been able to leave each other alone since the night of the storm. It was an obsession, this need to touch constantly. Everything they had done together had led to this desperate need for contact, to touch and caress with mouths and hands and legs entwined. Even preparing a meal together had taken an eternity because of this burning need to be wrapped in each other's arms.

Like now, when she couldn't resist the urge to smooth her palm across his chest, to reassure herself that he was real and not an illusion. Oh, God, she mouthed silently as she lowered her lips to his shoulder, just to feel his warmth and his firmness was like an aphrodisiac to her senses. But tomorrow they had to leave to go back to Grenada for the wedding. Dear God, that wedding; how could she have foreseen that fate would twist her heart so cruelly? On the way from Miami she had been wondering how she was going to cope with it, and that had been nothing to what she would have to cope with now. Would she lose Victor once they were back on Grenada? Was it true, all he'd said about paradise? Was this just an

oasis of passion in a desert of real life? Did Victor
love her with the same insatiability with which she
loved him?

'What are you thinking?' he murmured without
opening his eyes.

'I was thinking we have to go back tomorrow for
a wedding the day after,' she told him softly, twining
a strand of his hair between her fingers.

'It's a pain, isn't it?' he replied sleepily.

And that was all, Christie thought miserably. Had
she expected more? She didn't know, because this
paradise was so unreal, but what was very real was
that the day after the wedding she would be returning
to England, he to the States, and then what?

'We'd better get back and cook this fish before it
spoils,' she said sensibly, getting up and scrambling
back into her bikini. Some things were best blocked
out.

They were silent as Victor steered the boat back to
shore. They were silent as they prepared the fire on
the beach, wrapped the fish, and left it to bake in the
hot ashes while they went back to the house to shower
the salt from their bodies. And in silence they gave
in to the need that took over as they shared that
shower—the need to touch, to caress, as they soaped
each other's bodies. They didn't speak till Christie
was laying the table on the veranda ready for their
meal and Victor had collected the fish from its pyre
and brought it to the table.

'What did you mean the other day about Paul
bringing you into the family from the cold?'

He looked surprised that she had remembered that.
'The family had always known of my existence, but

Paul was the first to approach me. He'd heard I was a lawyer and wanted . . .' He didn't go on, just left the sentence in mid-air.

'And wanted what?' Christie urged, stopping what she was doing to look at him.

He looked away from her and went about breaking the fish into portions, and Christie had the feeling that he regretted what he had said, but she couldn't understand why she should get that feeling. It was something so subtle, so small, that she wondered if she was being over-sensitive. And she was feeling very sensitive, almost raw with the thought of leaving all this to return to the real world and its confusions.

'He was in the States a few years back and looked me up. Curiosity, I suspect, but we formed a good friendship and kept in touch.'

She watched him as he poured the wine. The sun would be going down soon and another day gone, and another day no nearer knowing what made him tick. She felt he was holding something back, and because of that rawness inside her she didn't pursue it.

'We're never going to able to eat all this,' he said as he filled their plates. 'It really was an excellent catch.'

His voice was toneless and Christie wondered if he was feeling the rawness too. He must be. Their time together had been ecstatic. He must know how she felt about him, but she didn't know for sure how deeply he felt for her. Yet that was an immature admission in itself, after all they had been to each other over the days. She couldn't help bringing back to mind how wrong she had been about Paul's feelings for her and about her own feelings for him at the time. She

had been wrong before, so there was no reason to
think she had learnt anything new. Except she had;
she'd learnt the difference between love and an infatuation. One man, one love. Victor was it.

Later that night they took a last moonlit stroll along
the beach. Victor was quiet, Christie was over the top
with contrived sparkling humour till she felt she was
getting very close to irritating him, but when they
returned to the wooden house they made love as if
for the first time, like that almost indecent haste
during the storm, that feverish rush of emotions, as
if they couldn't wait to get it over with because it was
causing such a barrier between them. And those barriers had crashed down after and they had been lost
in each other for a few idyllic days, but
now...somehow those barriers were coming up again.
Christie could feel it like a physical force rising between them. A safety barrier to prepare themselves
for the inevitable hurt of parting.

Victor slept immediately after and Christie slipped
out of bed to sit on the veranda in the darkness and
to will herself to hate him for his peace. But why
should she even consider that the hurt would be inevitable? Why couldn't it be moonlight and roses all
the way? Because paradise wasn't really like that...
And while she suffered an anguished uncertainty over
their future Victor slept. Her heart was tearing and
he slept. Her heart was raw with pain and he slept.
She wanted to die with the agony of it all and he slept.
She cried and he slept.

They spent the morning clearing up the house, Christie
putting on a false attitude of exuberance at the

prospect of returning to Grenada till the exuberance
died a death on her and worrying thoughts about Paul
and Michelle took over.

'What on earth are we going to find when we get
back?' she asked, though it was more an open musing
than a direct question.

She took Victor's computer and placed it carefully
next to her in the back of the boat. He hadn't allowed
her to help get the boat back in the water, saying it
was too heavy for her. He had worked as if the work
was a balm to him, the physical back-breaking effort
something to keep him occupied, rather than having
to talk to her.

It had been like that since breakfast, a struggle to
get a word out of him. Christie prayed that it was
because they were leaving and he just didn't know
what to say, but deep down she felt the truth knifing
her, stabbing away at her, not for the kill but a
lingering torture. It was the end, because if it wasn't
he'd have said by now. Silence sometimes said more
than words could. It upset her, desperately, but it annoyed her too, and yet in a way the silence was an
absurd relief. If they had opened up to each other she
might come out of it much worse than she was already
feeling. A bit of pride was worth hanging on to. If
he didn't want to speak of it she too would show her
maturity in just accepting it as such, an affair that
had to end.

'Paul and Michelle, you mean?' he asked absently.
'Yes.'

'What does it matter?' he said quietly as he piled
their bags on the deck.

'Don't be so unfeeling, Victor,' she said tightly. 'I just hope all this effort on our part was worth while, that they've managed to work things out.'

He spun to face her and said coldly, 'No. You wouldn't like to think the whole extravaganza was a total waste of time, would you?'

Christie was on her feet instantly, all good intentions of handling this with maturity swept aside in a rush of uncoolness. 'There's that damn word again..."extravaganza"...'

He stared at her for her outburst and then suddenly she was in his arms, flinging her arms around his neck and clinging to him blindly, and then the anger and the hurt poured out and she started to thump his back.

'Is that all I am, an extravaganza?' she sobbed. 'Oh, God, I hate you for that!'

He gripped her so hard that it hurt, and wrenched her away from him so he could look deep into her swimming eyes. 'Listen to me, Christie. I know what you're feeling. God knows I don't want this to end——'

Another sob caught in her throat and her words came out in a strangled rush. 'But...but it's going to, isn't it? We get...get back to Grenada and... and——'

'And we don't know what we are going to find. You said it yourself!' he grated fiercely. 'And I'm sorry if I sounded unfeeling when I said it didn't matter, but you're right, it does matter. Now listen to me.' His grip softened into a caress. 'These past few days have been the happiest of my life, you must believe that, but for the moment we must put our own feelings to rest for a while...'

Christie bit her lower lip so hard that she nearly drew blood.

'Paul and Michelle are going to need us. We don't know what has happened between them. The damned marriage could be off or on, we don't know. Soon we're going to find out, and for the time being their problems are uppermost, and besides...'

'Besides?' she whispered hoarsely, eyes so wide that they hurt.

His dark eyes were suddenly expressionless again. She hated it when he did that, closed off from her.

'We need a cooling-off period,' he breathed at last, his voice gravel in his throat.

Dear God...a 'cooling-off period', to give them time to think of what fools they had been?

Christie shrank away from him, overwhelmed by his cold common sense, and her pride stinging so badly that she was sick with it. She had shown her feelings so openly, made such a fool of herself. She shouldn't have flung herself at him like a lovesick teenager. She was a mature woman and should be able to take this with the same coolness he was—detached now, because it was all coming to an end. Their paradise madness was heading for sanity.

She slumped back in her seat, but Victor wouldn't allow the withdrawal, and hauled her up again to face him.

His mouth formed words and he spoke them with clarity. 'I'm even more crazy about you than I was when I first snatched those damned earphones from you, but Christie, darling, I can't make irrational promises——'

Her heart iced in defensive dismay. The deepest
fears of rejection were fuel for her anger. 'I'm not
asking for promises, Victor,' she blazed. 'God forbid
that I haven't seen this and taken it for exactly what
it was—a few days of passion and no strings——'

'I'm not saying that——'

'And I'm not hearing you deny it. You listen to *me*.
I can take it, Victor, because I was fully aware of what
I was letting myself in for from the off.' She fought
herself to show the same common sense as he, but it
was a monumental struggle. Deep down she was a
hurt female imploring him to love her and not cast
her out of his heart, but outside she was stiffened with
pride to cover the hurt. 'I don't want promises,' she
whispered, 'and I don't give them myself. I've had a
wonderful time with you, the very best, but I'm not...'

She couldn't even say it—looking for more. But
suddenly she knew what she had said was true, because now she was sane. They had known each other
for a handful of days, and you couldn't be hopelessly
in love after such a short space of time. Had she made
the same mistake again? Fool's paradise—this was it!

Oh, why hadn't she seen that before, that love grew
over a period of time, it didn't just come up and snap
at your heart so suddenly? He knew it, this Victor
who was so damned sensible; he knew it, and that was
what his silence had said. This wasn't love but
infatuation.

'But I'm not in love with you,' she finished strongly,
so strongly that she thought—no, imagined—
he'd flinched.

He let her go and she was so weak with what she was forcing herself to believe that she slumped again, back into the seat he had just hauled her up from.

'That makes it easier, Christie,' he said quietly, before turning away to fire the engine of the boat.

All the way back to Grenada she watched the back of him, so hurt that her eyes were tearless. Yes, how easy that made it for him to drop her as swiftly as he had lifted her. He believed she didn't love him, and that must make for an easy conscience for him.

There was no one around the hotel on their return. Victor made no comment about the silence, and she supposed he presumed that everyone was taking a siesta. Odd, but Christie felt an unease. It was the time for siesta, but there was something intangible about the stillness of the hotel, an underlying foreboding.

'Do you feel something?' Victor asked as they walked along the garden pathway to their suites.

Christie looked at him in surprise. 'I didn't think you'd noticed.'

Their eyes met for a brief second and Christie looked away. Such a short time they had known each other, but already their minds were in tune.

Victor put her bag down on her entrance terrace. 'I'll go and take a look around. I don't like the feel of things.'

'I'll come with you.'

Victor's hand touched her wrist lightly and he gave her a small smile, the first for so long. 'Go and take a rest.' Suddenly his hand came up and smoothed her tousled hair from her face. 'You look as if you've been ravaged.'

She forced a smile herself, because it was the only way. 'I have been, thoroughly.'

'Yes,' he murmured. 'I think I know something about that.'

Their eyes locked again and Christie felt her heart thud with hope, and then he turned quickly away and said over his shoulder, 'I'll let you know what I find out.'

Christie closed the door after him, leant against it wearily, and closed her eyes. She wanted so desperately to cry for everything that wasn't going to be, but the tears were forced back by this unease that niggled inside her. There was something wrong here at the hotel, the silence unnatural.

Slowly she unpacked and then, to fill time till Victor returned, she washed out her clothes, took a cool shower and shampooed her hair, and then sat out on the terrace to dry it naturally, flicking her fingers through it, wondering and wondering what was keeping Victor.

Christie waited and waited, pacing up and down, until she could stand it no longer. She had to find out for herself what was going on.

The storm must have hit Grenada as well as the tiny island they had been on. The gardens were as lush as ever, but some of the exotic flowers had been dashed to the ground with the force of the wind and the rain. The shore looked as if it had been newly combed, though, as if it had been covered in debris and the hotel had made an effort to put it all back in pristine order.

Suddenly a cold chill ran through Christie and she stopped dead on her way to Hotel Reception along the beach path. She'd been on holiday in the Bahamas a few years before, a tiny secluded island where she had arrived just after a small hurricane had hit it. Palm trees had keeled over and the beach had been stripped of sand in parts and was down to bare rock. A small beachfront hotel had caught the main force and there had been fatalities and many injured.

Christie was immobilised for a few seconds, wondering if there had been a hurricane here and they, on their tiny paradise island, had only received the tail-end of it. Oh, dear God, this could explain that strange silence, that strange eerie silence of recovery.

She broke into a run, her heart thudding with fear, her mind spinning with conjecture. She could see her cousin, Michelle, injured by a falling roof...Paul...lying in the rubble of collapsing masonry...the other wedding guests dazed and stunned with shock at the turbulence of a tropical storm.

Christie slowed her pace. This was ridiculous. There were no visible signs of any collapsed buildings, and besides, the taxi driver from the marina would have said. The West Indians held nothing back. Hell, she couldn't even recall what he had been talking to Victor about on the way to back to the hotel. She'd been that wrapped up in her own selfish, miserable thoughts that she hadn't listened.

She reached Reception, hot and perspiring. The hurricane theory loomed again as she noticed there were no other guests anywhere in sight. The hotel was still in one piece—built out of coral stone, it would have held up against a war—but the outside suites, the cottages in the grounds...

'Yes, ma'am, we had plenty of rain, welcome too.' The young man on Reception grinned at her anguished query. 'No hurricane, though.'

Christie's heart eased and a flood of relief had her grinning like a Cheshire cat.

'But...but where is everyone?'

'The wedding guests left two days ago——'

'Left?' Christie cried, her head spinning with the implications of that. 'What do you mean, "left"?'

The receptionist shrugged his shoulders, but the grin was perpetual. 'Just upped and left.'

'Everyone?' Christie exclaimed. 'But the bride and the groom...I mean, they were going to be married...'

'I don't know nothing, ma'am, just that they all left in a hurry. The only ones left are Miss Michelle and——'

'And Paul, Paul Tarrat, the bridegroom?'

Please don't say that he's gone too, Christie prayed. She'd never be able to cope with that. The guilt would be too much to bear. She should never have allowed herself to be persuaded away by Victor. Had Paul left Michelle all alone with no one to turn to?

'Mr Tarrat didn't leave with the others, but he's not in the hotel at the moment. He drove into St George's this morning and hasn't been back. Is there anything I can help you with?'

'No...no, thank you.'

Christie headed straight for Michelle's suite on the other side of the hotel, taking the beach route for quickness. She felt sick with worry. Why had all the guests left? What an earth had happened in their absence? The place was so damned empty that it was eerie.

A soft, heart-shuddering moan escaped Christie's lips as she rounded the coral wall by the hotel terrace where most of the pre-wedding gaiety had taken place, the wall where she had sat and Paul had fed her prawns, the place where Victor had watched her so suspiciously. Now Christie watched with eyes that burned with tears and anger, and her heart tore with such fearful jealousy that she nearly screamed her anguish out across the blue, blue sea.

The beach wasn't empty. Two figures stood by the edge of the tranquil water, framed against the horizon, but not in silhouette, against the backdrop of a moon-silvered sea. The sun was cruel in lighting the two people wrapped in each other's arms, oh, so cruel and no friend to Christie.

She stepped back till she was pressed painfully against the low wall, behind a hibiscus shrub, and out of sight of the two lovers who were so wrapped up in each other that they wouldn't have noticed if a circus were performing in front of them.

And it was all a circus, Christie cried inwardly, not even an extravaganza. A sordid little circus where Victor had run rings round her till she was skipping through hoops of flames.

Never in all her life had she felt so cheated, so used, so abandoned. In that moment of despair she hated everyone on this paradise wedding island, but more than anything she hated Victor Lascelles for standing down on that beach with his arms wrapped lovingly around her cousin, showing the world where his heart truly lay.

CHAPTER NINE

THROUGH a blur of tears Christie stumbled back to her suite, through the perfumed gardens, past the spot where she had sat with Victor, past everything that was a painful reminder of that man.

'Christie!'

Christie swung round in panic, for a second not recognising the voice.

'Paul,' she cried and only just stopped throwing herself in his arms. In that blinding second of recognition at the sight of him a small part of her heart bled for him too. The wedding was off and he must be feeling so wretched. How was he taking it, the treachery of his own cousin and Michelle?

'Christie, darling.' He drew her into his arms and she held him fiercely. 'Oh, thank God you're back. We've been through hell here. You were best out of it, I promise you.'

He released her and Christie stepped back, taking in the strained features of his face. She opened her mouth to speak, to somehow try and find the words of consolation she felt she ought to offer, but the words didn't come because Paul's mouth suddenly broke into a grin.

'I'll mix you a drink and tell you all about it.'

Hands shaking, Christie opened the door of her suite, and while Paul headed for the courtesy bar Christie struggled for her sanity. Paul looked terrible, so was that last grin a brave attempt at normality after all he had been through? Perhaps she might gain some strength from him. If he could cope, maybe she could too. But no, she couldn't; she'd never be able to come to terms with this terrible loss.

'So everyone has left,' Christie said heavily as she took the gin and tonic he had poured her. Her hand was shaking as she took it, and she perversely thought he hadn't even noticed. It was a totally selfish thought. Why should Paul be remotely concerned about what she might have been through these past few days when he'd been through so much himself? This was his shout, anyway, this wedding that wasn't going to happen, and she had no right to expect sympathy for her own predicament.

'I sent them back. It all got out of hand. It was clouding so many issues, all this boozing and dancing the nights away. Michelle and I couldn't think straight.' He flopped down in one of the sofas and grinned sheepishly. 'I made a fool of myself with you, Christie, and for that I apologise. When you went off with Victor I was able to think a bit straighter.' He leaned forward, cradled his drink in his hands, and looked up at her. 'It's not easy, you know, this marriage thing. We did it all wrong. We shouldn't have come here. We should have stayed home and done it the conventional way.'

'Yes,' Christie murmured, staring down at her drink, badly needing it but knowing nausea would follow because you couldn't drink on top of what she felt and expect it all to be numbed away.

'Anyway, it's too late now,' Paul went on.

Christie lifted her eyes. 'I'm so sorry, Paul, truly sorry, but maybe it was for the best coming out here anyway. It could have happened back in England with all the family around, and that would have been worse——'

He wasn't even listening. 'Michelle was furious with you for going away with Victor...'

Christie's insides rebelled at that. She bet she was. Anger bubbled again, this time directed at Michelle for her deceit and utter selfishness. She could hardly believe it of her, but love made you do silly things. Christie knew that.

'She needed you here, Christie——'

'As she needed a hole in her pretty little head,' Christie repeated in a muted whisper as she made for the open patio doors for some much needed fresh air.

'But on reflection you two did us a favour, disappearing like that. We had to thrash it out between us the best way we could, and I suppose it was the only way. We really opened up to each other about our uncertainty and fears. Once the others were out of the way as well it made it a lot easier. We were able to rediscover each other. Another drink?'

Paul was at the bar before Christie could stop him. She swivelled from the doors and looked at him in amazement. Rediscover each other?

'We're stronger now, Christie,' he went on, 'more sure of ourselves and how we feel about each other. We've been to hell and back and fortunately landed in one piece——'

'Just...just a minute,' Christie faltered, her eyes wide and dismayed. 'You're...you're not going through with this?'

He laughed and glanced at her with surprise. 'Of course, that's what we came here for—to be married. Slightly different arrangements; just the two of you as wedding guests now, and really that's the way it should be...'

The room spun for Christie; the ice in her drink clattered against the sides of her glass as her hand shook with the impact of what Paul was saying. He didn't know! Paul didn't know about Michelle and Victor and he was going ahead with the wedding!

Paul came and stood beside her to gaze out over the whirlpool and the tranquil sea and horizon beyond.

'I love her so much, Christie, and it's a funny thing, but I'm glad we had those doubts, because we've come out of it with a love that is so much stronger. I know we're doing the right thing now.' He gave out a contented sigh of well-being. 'Life couldn't be better. I'm going to marry the woman I love and then we're going to have a glorious honeymoon, and when we get back to England I'm going to expand the business...'

Oh, there was more of Paul's 'glorious' expectations of life, but Christie didn't listen. His words blurred around her ears till they were a drone in the background. She lifted the glass to her lips and for the first time drank thirstily, wanting life to blur out...but suddenly...suddenly and painfully a snatch of his conversation got through the barrier of her hurt.

'W-what did you say?'

'I thought he would have told you.' Paul laughed. 'I want Victor as the company lawyer and caught him just at the right time. He's ready for a change of direction, restless with the divorce market and wanting to stretch his talents and expand his agency; besides, it's time my father recognised him as one of the family. We've been talking about it for a couple of months now. Victor is winding up his affairs in the States and will be joining us in England.'

Christie swallowed the rest of her drink, turned away from Paul, and poured herself another. She couldn't form a thought without it, but the drink remained in her hand, fused to her hot fingers as she gripped it fiercely. So Victor was going to set up in England, was he? To be near Michelle, to carry on this revolting affair, even though she was going to be married to his cousin! She couldn't bear it; she wouldn't bear it!

'And you, Christie, how did it all go with Victor? I couldn't believe it when I got the message he left.' He shook his head in amazement. 'I was only joking when I suggested you two get it together, didn't think for a minute he would take it quite so literally.'

The numbness took over then and Christie knew she couldn't be hurt any more than she was already. Was it so unlikely to everyone that Victor could be attracted to her? Obviously so.

Paul moved away from the doors and put his empty glass down on the bar. 'I'll go and tell Michelle you're back. She'll be thrilled.'

'Funny she wasn't when I left,' Christie muttered, loud enough for Paul to hear.

Paul laughed. 'That was then. She needed you then.'

And now she doesn't, Christie thought ruefully, and Paul wasn't really interested in how she had got on with his cousin; he hadn't even pursued the question.

She couldn't feel sorry for him or anyone any more.
There was only enough sorrow left for herself.

Christie was in no condition to tackle Victor when he
eventually came to her suite some time after Paul had
left. She was in the middle of packing, working like
someone brain dead from over-exposure to too many
conflicting emotions. She'd suffered them all—anger,
despair, jealousy and some thousand others besides—
so when she let Victor in she had to force immense
calm. The effort made her feel that insanity was fast
developing and would be welcome, too.

'Paul said he'd seen you, so I guess you know that
all's well that ends well.'

He looked a little strained around the mouth and
eyes and she supposed that in the circumstances he
was allowed it. There was even a smile for him as she
ushered him in.

'Yes, quite a relief,' she remarked tonelessly. 'Would
you like a drink?' She poured him one without waiting
for an answer, but not one for herself; she didn't need
it any more.

'They want us to join them for dinner tonight and
I accepted for us both.' He sat on the sofa, but not
at ease, and took the drink from her.

Another smile. She *was* insane.

'That will be nice,' she said.

It wouldn't be nice at all—she could think of
nothing worse—but she wouldn't be here, so what did
it matter what she said? She perched herself on the
arm of the other sofa and looked at him. She was icy-
cold and not even the look of him, slightly harassed
handsome, could warm her.

'Paul seems very happy; how about Michelle?'

She expected a denial that he'd seen her, and was honestly surprised when none came.

'Not such a clear case of knowing your inner self,' he mused, staring down at his drink.

'Oh.'

'I don't think I was much help,' he said on a sigh. 'I think it's over to you now. She needs a woman to talk to.'

Slowly Christie got up and poured herself a drink, needing it now, but what she didn't need was her cousin pouring her heart out to her, asking her advice on whether she was doing the right thing, when it was blatantly obvious that if you were having an affair with the best man you wouldn't be doing the right thing by marrying the groom!

Except that . . . Christie closed her eyes as her heart started to thump in her breast, so loudly that it thudded in her ears. Oh, God, what was happening to her? What on earth was she thinking of? Slowly she opened her eyes and looked at Victor as he stared broodingly into his drink. This man she had shared four idyllic days with on an idyllic tropical island surely couldn't be capable of anything so despicable. Could that fond embrace she had witnessed have been just that, a fond embrace of consolation rather than the passion of two lovers reunited? Oh, God, was it possible that she had misconstrued the whole poignant scene, as she had once before?

In that instant she knew she had, and the feeling wasn't good, not good at all, because it brought such a flood of new feelings about herself that she hardly dared face them. Was she really so shallow? She didn't even have enough faith in her own feelings for Victor and his for her and what had passed between them on that secret island to come up with a good, honest explanation for why he should have been holding Michelle that way on the beach. She'd thought the worst because that was all she was capable of, thinking the very worst of everyone and everything.

'She...she's still having doubts?' Christie asked tremulously.

'She loves him, I'm convinced of that, but she's uncertain of herself. Hard to imagine such a bubbly, open sort of person not being able to come to terms with her own feelings and accept them.'

Christie nearly laughed out loud at the irony of that.

Victor looked across at her and met her eyes. 'I think you should listen to her, because I've done all I can and it isn't enough.' He paused and his eyes took on a new depth of meaning. 'I want all this out of the way, Christie, because to be frank I'm sick of the whole business. I came down here for a wedding——'

'And it does rather interfere with your work, doesn't it?' she interrupted sarcastically.

Immediately she'd said that it added weight to what she had just been thinking about herself—that she was incapable of forming a rational thought about anything any more. She couldn't even hold a normal, sensible conversation with this man without making a mess of it and acting with such stupid immaturity that she made herself cringe.

'I'm sorry, I shouldn't have said that; it was out of order.' She paused and lowered her eyes. 'I'm not going to give her a shoulder to cry on, Victor,' she added soberly, 'because I too am sick of the whole damn extravaganza.'

She put her glass down on the bar with a thump. She was angry with herself, disappointed in herself, and contrarily angry with him because he was incapable of making her feel safe and secure. If he had any feelings for her why couldn't he show them? She was about to storm off to her bedroom, to be alone to think, when he caught her and swung her to face him.

'You are; she needs you, and then hopefully this damn *extravaganza* will be done and finished with and we can try and sort out our own problems.'

'Oh, we have some, do we?' she grated fiercely, tensing her shoulders in his grip. 'I don't see that, no, I don't at all. We have no problems, Victor, because to have problems you have to have some sort of a relationship to have them in, and we haven't! It's a pity you couldn't have taught Michelle what you have taught me, to know oneself——'

His eyes darkened with anger. 'You're far from knowing yourself, Christie; that's the whole damned *problem*——'

'Huh, that's where you're wrong! I've learnt one helluva a lot about myself in the past three minutes, as it happens. I've learnt that I'm absolutely hopeless at relationships, that I'm incapable of having a decent thought about anyone, least of all myself, and all because...because of you, damn you!' The tears came then, big fat blobs of childish tears. With one enormous wrench she was free from him and across the room, pushing her bedroom door open and wanting to slam it in his face.

Victor followed, and caught the door before it hit
him. He stopped dead in the doorway and Christie
turned. Her misty eyes widened as his darkened
threateningly at the sight of her suitcase packed on
the bed.

'What's that?' he grated.

'What does it damned well look like?' she croaked
through a sob.

'It's full.'

'Yes, it's full. I've no intention of leaving anything
behind.'

'Don't be so childish!'

He crossed the room and snatched out the cream
lace dress she had intended wearing for the wedding.
He threw it down on the bed as if it were trash and
turned to her angrily, a dark infusion of colour rising
from his neck.

'What is it with you?'

'And what is it with you?' she cried back, and then
her insides seem to fold in on her. 'Oh, God!' she
moaned and slumped down on the edge of the bed
and covered her face with her hands. 'I'm twenty-
five,' she sobbed. 'I'm acting like a kid and I can't
stop it and I hate it, I hate it!'

She felt the pressure of him sitting next to her on
the bed and then his arm coming around her shoulder,
and she leaned against him and knew his anger had
dissipated and he was as confused as her.

'I . . . I was going to leave now, tonight,' she cried.
'I didn't want to be here for the wedding... I wouldn't
have been able to bear it ... I thought...' No, she
couldn't tell him what she thought—that he was still
romantically involved with Michelle. Still? He never

had been in the first place! She loathed herself for that; it pounded into her already bruised senses how totally useless she was at affairs of the heart. She couldn't even allow herself to trust. But what was there to trust in Victor? Why hadn't he told her he was moving to England? Was it because he couldn't make any 'irrational promises' to her, like wanting to carry on this crazy whirlwind affair once they left the Caribbean?

'Paul...Paul said...' she started, but Victor stilled her words by turning her to face him. His face was grave.

'I don't want to hear anything Paul has said,' he grated roughly. He tilted her chin and grazed his lips across hers, and she was so very nearly lost.

'Don't do that, Victor,' she breathed. 'It doesn't change anything.'

'Well, something's got to change or we're doomed, Christie.' This time his mouth was more assertive, and how easy it would be to let him make love to her, spin her back into that sense of unreality she had been floating on these past days. But they weren't on that secret island any more, and harsh reality was biting into her reserves of strength.

'I am going,' she murmured determinedly against his mouth. 'I really am, because I'm sick of putting other people's feelings ahead of my own.'

'And what about mine?' he husked against her cheek.

She tensed with the pain. 'You ... you haven't any.'

He held her firmly, feeling the tension. 'I have and I've made them clear to you, as clear as I'm able to at the moment.'

'And it doesn't matter,' she breathed quietly, so in control now that it was almost frightening. She eased him away from her, far enough to look into his eyes. 'Victor, I want to go, because it will hurt too much to stay and ... and I want to tell you why.'

'I know why.' His hand came up to smooth the tears from her face. 'You don't have to tell me, because I know. You hurt me so deeply when you denied you loved me on the boat, but now I know why you said it—to save your pride. It's why I haven't said the things you want to hear, because I have my pride too. Neither of us wants to be hurt and you're as scared as I am.'

She opened her mouth to deny that, but what was there to deny? It was all true, but there was more, so much more, so much more uncertainty she wanted to tell him about, but the words didn't blossom because he wouldn't allow them to.

'I'm terrified of losing you,' he told her passionately. 'I'm terrified you don't care enough about me to want to stay and talk this out. I can't even form those words I know you want to hear, because that fear of rejection is all at the moment. Those irrational promises I mentioned I can't make, because I'm so uncertain about you. I've led a life where I thought I was in control, and now I'm not. I've never allowed a woman into my life because I've never met one I've cared deeply enough about to allow in, not until now and you. I've seen my mother make a screaming mess of her life and I'm terrified of making the same mistakes. I want you and I don't. I hate you for the power you have over me and yet I love you for that power. I'm shocked that in four days you have completely unbalanced my life.' He stopped and held her chin, rubbing his thumb along it, not in a caress but more in a gesture of defiance. 'I want to make love to you, now, because when I'm doing that I don't have to think of anything else but our own sweet pleasure. Do you want to hear more?'

Bemused, confused, she stared at him in shock.

'I...I know it all,' she breathed raggedly. Wasn't it everything she had felt herself since meeting him? The confusion, the pain, the agony of loving and not understanding that loving. 'And...and it doesn't help, Victor.' She shook her head with the shame of that admission. 'And...and we don't have anyone to turn to——'

'Only ourselves, Christie, and if we can't find the answers within ourselves we haven't a chance. But we owe it to ourselves to try.'

She lowered her head and gave a very small smile to her lap. 'I don't even know how to begin.'

'You can try telling me what I've just more or less told you—that you love me as I love you.'

Remarkable, but it didn't even register properly. She should feel elated at the admission, but she didn't. It was all to do with this awful feeling inside her, this almost dream-like quality to everything around her. She felt suspended in time, floating, uncertain of where she was going to land and afraid that, wherever it was, it still wouldn't be right.

'I know I said I didn't love you. You were right, I denied it to save my pride, but...' She looked up at him. 'But you must have known,' she whispered.

'And you must have known I loved you too.'

Shame gripped her then. Yes, she should have known.

'I love you, Victor,' she said quietly, her eyes brimming with tears once again. She gave a very tremulous shrug of her shoulders. 'You see,' she whispered softly, 'it doesn't help, because what sort of love can it be when I thought you were having an affair with Michelle?' Her eyes focused on his through the wash of tears. 'Not four days ago, but now, a while back when I saw the two of you on the beach, wrapped so lovingly in each other's arms...'

'Not wrapped so lovingly, Christie, simply comforting someone who needed it at the time.'

'I know that now; I've worked it out for myself. You were consoling her, trying to help her in the only way you could, by giving your support, as you were that night she was in your suite. I know all that now and in a way I understand why you didn't tell me you were coming to England. You're so unsure of us that you wanted to leave yourself space to get out of all this if it didn't work out. When Paul told me you were going to set up in England and be his company lawyer my first thought was that you were doing it for Michelle, and, you see, that is the whole crippling problem, this uncertainty I feel. For an instant I doubted you and myself. If I could think that of you, what hope was there for us?'

Christie lifted her hands and ran them tenderly down the sides of his face. 'Victor, on the strength of four days of love and passion we can't possibly make any irrational promises to each other.'

'Exactly,' he said, and there was a small smile on the edge of his lips that she didn't understand. 'I'm glad you came to that conclusion of your own free will,' he said tenderly. 'Now before we take us and our emotions a step further, will you do me a small favour and go and have that chat with Michelle? Girls' talk.'

She didn't understand that—why he should make such a suggestion when they and their feelings were far more important at the moment.

'I can't, Victor,' she breathed. 'How can I offer Michelle any advice when I'm so confused myself?'

'You don't give advice, remember, you just listen— and you will. I have every faith in you and I want you to do it. Please do it for me, Christie, darling.'

He lowered his lips to hers and the kiss was so tender and loving and persuasive that she felt her whole heart melting under the sweet pressure. He didn't know it, but she would do anything for him, and this small favour was so very unimportant, but once out of the way perhaps they could work something out for themselves, perhaps they could find the time and space to give to each other.

'Yes, I'll go,' she told him at last as he drew back from her.

His enigmatic smile was all that he offered to speed her on her way.

On the way to Michelle's suite she told herself a hundred times that she was ill equipped for helping Michelle to come to a decision about her future when her own was in such a tangle. But what was it Victor had said about the first rule of counselling and had just reminded her of? Just listen. That wouldn't take much effort on her part. She had little else to offer;

certainly no words of wisdom would flow from her inexperienced lips.

Michelle fell on her when she answered the door.

'Oh, God, I've missed you,' she gasped, hugging her so tightly that she nearly drew off Christie's last breath. 'What am I going to do, Christie? I love him, I really do, but I'm so scared, so terrified of making a mistake... Paul loves me too, I'm sure of that now... He's so certain . . . certain that he wants to marry me, but . . .'

There was more, so much outpouring of uncertainties that Christie nearly blanked off from it all. They echoed so much of how she felt herself that it hurt to listen.

Michelle opened a bottle of ice-cold champagne and shakily poured two glasses, and poured her heart out with it.

Christie sat across from her and listened to the outpourings till the sun went down and there was just the glow from a tropical sun firing the sky crimson and gold and purple in its last death throes as it sizzled into the Caribbean sea.

'Christie, you're crying.' At last Michelle stopped and suddenly she was beside her cousin, hugging her to her. 'What's wrong? Tell me what's wrong.'

Christie lifted her head and smiled through her tears. She looked at her dear cousin, her silly blind cousin, and sniffed so loudly that they both laughed a little uncertainly.

'Oh, there's nothing wrong, nothing at all.' Somehow the fog had cleared and the truth was exposed for Christie to rejoice in, the glorious truth that just needed to be accepted. 'Listen to me, Micky, dear.

I'm breaking all the rules here, but I don't care. I've listened to all your doubts and fears and now I'm going to tell you what to do.' She sniffed again and wiped the back of her hand across her eyes and smiled again. Michelle watched her, puzzled, eyes wide in expectation.

Christie gripped her hand tightly and took a deep breath. 'It's really very easy when you know how,' she told her. 'Quite, quite simple. All you do is ask yourself a few simple questions. Can you live without him?'

'Oh, no,' Michelle breathed shakily, her eyes wide with pain at the thought. 'No, I couldn't... I want him and need him.'

Christie smiled and sniffed again. 'Do you want to spend the rest of your life with him?'

Michelle looked at her as if she were crazy. 'Yes... yes, of course I do.'

Christie nodded, in her heart answering the very same questions for herself. 'And are you prepared to put up with some of his infuriating habits?'

'Oh, he hasn't got any.' Then she laughed. 'Well, only a few, and yes... yes, I can live with them.'

Christie stood up and looked down on her cousin, gave a very dismissive shrug of her shoulders, held out her palms, and beamed a broad smile. 'That's it, Michelle. It's as simple as that.'

'But... but...'

'No buts, Michelle. They're all behind you now. You love each other and that's all, absolutely all that is important.'

Michelle smiled, and the anguish and the uncertainty faded away with it, and her eyes sparkled again.

'You know, that's what Victor said, but he didn't sound so sure as you do.'

'Perhaps because he wasn't sure, but I'm sure he's sure now.'

So wrapped up in her own happiness was Michelle that she didn't query that mysterious statement, and Christie was glad. She didn't want to talk about it, not with her cousin, but she needed to talk about it with the man she loved.

Christie knew exactly where he would be, but she didn't hasten her pace to join him. For a while she wanted to cherish this new feeling inside her. She wanted to enjoy this love wrapping itself around her heart, sealing out all the doubts and worries and uncertainties. It was such a good feeling, a sort of winging freedom of spirit. Four minutes, four hours, four days, four months, for life! She knew with a positiveness that was a joy to behold that she loved Victor Lascelles and always would, and she was going to tell him again and again, because he needed releasing too.

He stood on the edge of the water, staring across to the last fiery flames of an orange sun sinking low and swiftly into a molten gold sea. He stood pensive, solitary, hands plunged deep into the pockets of his linen trousers.

Slowly she went across the warm sand towards him and then she stopped, fighting the urge to fling herself at him and hold him, never to let him go.

'Can you live without me?' she murmured behind him, not wanting to touch him, not yet.

He didn't move, not a muscle. 'It would be impossible,' he said in a low voice. Still he didn't turn to face her, but his shoulders stiffened slightly. 'Can you live without me?'

'It would be impossible,' she repeated and drew a new breath of happiness as she saw his shoulders let go of the tension. 'Do you want to spend the rest of your life with me?'

'Without a doubt.' Slowly he withdrew his hands from his pockets. 'Do you want to spend the rest of your life with me?'

'Without a doubt,' she murmured truthfully.

He turned then and with a small sob she hurled herself at him, flung her arms around his neck, and held him tightly to her. His arms slid around her and he mouthed kisses of relief into her warm silken hair.

'You knew, didn't you?' Christie cried, covering his face with kisses. 'You knew that if I listened to Michelle it would clear the dross of my own uncertainties. Oh, I listened, Victor, how I listened. I listened so hard that I wanted to scream in the end. I wanted to slap her and shake her and tell her not to be so stupid and then...and then I remembered those questions you said you would ask yourself when you fell in love and I gave them to Michelle, but really...really I was asking myself them.'

Victor laughed and drew her hair back from her face with both hands, and looked deep into her eyes. 'I did too, my darling, way back in this whirlwind relationship of ours, but there were two sides to those questions and you were so confused you couldn't have given a lucid answer to what you wanted for breakfast, let alone what you wanted for our future.'

'Is...is that the only reason you held back from me?' she pleaded to know. 'All that about irrational promises, not telling me you were coming to England——'

'All the same fears and uncertainties you were going through, my love. I gave my heart far too soon and it shook me.'

'Me too,' she whispered. 'I was so knotted up with thoughts that I'd made such a mistake with Paul that I was terrified of making them all over again. Though I knew I loved you I doubted myself. But now I don't. I don't care about the fact that we've only known each other such a tiny, tiny while——'

'How many days is it?' He laughed.

Christie laughed with him and kissed his lips. 'Who's counting? It's not the length of time, but the intensity of feeling you pack into it. I've been through every emotion, Victor; you name it, I've done it. Jealousy was the one that said most. That night when I caught you with Michelle in your suite, it was jealousy that hit me the hardest, and, do you know, I was even jealous of Delia——?'

'Delia is fifty-eight, beautiful, yes, but a little too old for me, and I've been jealous, too, of Paul and what I thought you had going with him. It's why I gave you all those warnings.'

'They weren't needed, Victor.' She frowned suddenly. 'You know, you never did tell me what he told you that first night, about us being ex-lovers. I mean, he didn't actually say it, did he?'

'Not exactly. When he was telling me about you as we walked up from the beach he said he'd been close to you and, coupled with all his doubts about this wedding, it came across as if he'd had a deeper relationship and was regretting the passing of you. I honestly did believe you had been that close, till I got to know you better.'

'And you were jealous?'

'Madly; it's when I knew I was in trouble. So you see it isn't a woman's prerogative.' He stroked her chin suddenly and his mouth softened. 'And what the hell are we doing wasting our time talking about things that don't matter any more? I'd much rather be talking about the future than the past.'

'And tomorrow is the future,' Christie murmured happily, 'and one day that will be the past . . .'

'And then we'll talk about it because it will be *our* past and no one else's. I love you, Christie Vaughan, past, present and future.'

His kiss confirmed it, a kiss power-packed with love and desire and a certainty of the promise it held.

They drew back at last, deeply aroused and wanting so much more. Victor gazed down at the desire in her eyes and brought her down to earth.

'We have a dinner to attend; we'd better go.'

Christie sighed regretfully. 'With the wedding couple, yes. I suppose we'd better get ready.'

Victor ran his fingers lightly over the cleavage that peeked over her pareu. 'I'll help you undress,' he murmured suggestively as he took her hand as they started to stroll back up the beach.

'That would be nice,' she murmured longingly. 'Have we got time?'

Victor laughed and quickened the pace till they were running. 'We'll make time.'

And they did. Victor took her in his arms as soon as he kicked shut the door of his suite behind them.

'I love you so much it hurts,' he murmured as he unknotted her pareu and let it slide to the floor. He lowered his mouth to her nipples and drew on them tenderly and then drew back to look deep into her love-washed eyes.

'And I love you so much it hurts too, a pain I want to endure till the end of time,' she whispered, peeling his shirt from his shoulders to nestle her lips on his bare flesh.

'And we will,' he promised as he scooped her up and on to the bed. And with delicious unhurried calm they started to make love, each movement, each caress, each love-moist deep, penetrating thrust a testimony to the truth of that promise. Slowly, sensually, Victor pulsed her higher and higher till the hurt of uncertainty was washed away on a flood of heated delirium that had only one end, that ecstatic finale that left them drained and sated and mellowed into a sweet, sweet pleasure of certainty, a certainty of one man, one love, one woman, one love.

Christie took off her earphones and turned to her travelling companion as he tapped away on his computer. Concorde was whisking them from New York to Heathrow, and the journey's end couldn't come quick enough for Christie.

She fidgeted and the man next to her gave her his attention, turning to grin at her.

'Heathrow?' he asked.

Christie looked stoically ahead at the headrest in front of her. It was unavoidable, she supposed, getting chatted up by the best-looking bore on the flight.

'If not, I'm on the wrong flight. I'm going to a wedding actually,' she said stiffly.

'A wedding, eh?'

'Yes, a perfectly romantic wedding in Dorset.'

Nothing from her travelling companion.

She persisted. 'Yes, a perfectly romantic wedding in paradise. My own.'

'Hmm. Is this one for real?'

Christie grinned happily and held up her left hand, and gazed in rapture at the huge solitaire diamond on the third finger. 'It had better be real for the money you shelled out for it.'

She leaned across and kissed her travelling companion full on the lips. 'I love you, Victor Lascelles, and I can't wait to be your wife.'

'And I love you, Christie Vaughan, and I can't wait for you to be my wife.' He kissed the tip of her nose and then gently put the earphones back on her head and turned up the volume and went back to his computer. And Christie didn't mind at all.

Next Month's Romances

Each month you can choose from a wide variety of romance with Mills & Boon. Below are the new titles to look out for next month, why not ask either Mills & Boon Reader Service or your Newsagent to reserve you a copy of the titles you want to buy – just tick the titles you would like and either post to Reader Service or take it to any Newsagent and ask them to order your books.

Please save me the following titles: Please tick ✓

Title	Author	
PASSION'S MISTRESS	Helen Bianchin	
THE UPSTAIRS LOVER	Emma Darcy	
BODY AND SOUL	Charlotte Lamb	
WAITING FOR DEBORAH	Betty Neels	
WILDFIRE	Sandra Field	
IN NAME ONLY	Diana Hamilton	
AN IMPORTED WIFE	Rosalie Ash	
BLAMELESS DESIRE	Jenny Cartwright	
MASTER OF DESTINY	Sally Heywood	
DANCE TO THE DEVIL'S TUNE	Lucy Keane	
LIVING FOR LOVE	Barbara McMahon	
DARK AVENGER	Alex Ryder	
WHEN STRANGERS MEET	Shirley Kemp	
PAST IMPERFECT	Kristy McCallum	
JACINTH	Laurey Bright	
HEIR TO GLENGYLE	Miriam Macgregor	

If you would like to order these books in addition to your regular subscription from Mills & Boon Reader Service please send £1.90 per title to: Mills & Boon Reader Service, Freepost, P.O. Box 236, Croydon, Surrey, CR9 9EL, quote your Subscriber No:.................................... (If applicable) and complete the name and address details below. Alternatively, these books are available from many local Newsagents including W H Smith, J Menzies, Martins and other paperback stockists from 13 May 1994.

Name:..

Address:..

....Post Code:...........................

To Retailer: If you would like to stock M&B books please contact your regular book/magazine wholesaler for details.

You may be mailed with offers from other reputable companies as a result of this application. If you would rather not take advantage of these opportunities please tick box ☐